W9-BUL-644

THE TALLCHIEFS
Bestselling author Cait London's miniseries continues with Book 2
TALLCHIEF'S BRIDE

One long-ago night the five newly orphaned Tallchief children—Duncan, Calum, Elspeth, Birk and Fiona—vowed to stay together, to keep their home on Tallchief Mountain. They remembered their great-great-grandmother, who had sold off her wedding dowry to keep the Mountain in the family. To find courage and to honor hers, each child pledged to find one of the missing heirlooms and return it to the Tallchiefs.

This past June, Silhouette Desire brought you Book 1 of The Tallchiefs miniseries, *The Cowboy and the Cradle* (6/96 D#1006), in which Duncan reclaimed the baby cradle. Now, in *Tallchief's Bride*, Calum will find the missing ring—and with it, true love....

THE TALLCHIEFS: One family finds the love that legends—and little ones—are made of.

Dear Reader,

Established stars and exciting new names...that's what's in store for you this month from Silhouette Desire. Let's begin with Cait London's MAN OF THE MONTH, *Tallchief's Bride*—it's also the latest in her wonderful series, THE TALLCHIEFS.

The fun continues with *Babies by the Busload,* the next book in Raye Morgan's THE BABY SHOWER series, and *Michael's Baby,* the first installment of Cathie Linz's delightful series, THREE WEDDINGS AND A GIFT.

So many of you have indicated how much you love the work of Peggy Moreland, so I know you'll all be excited about her latest sensuous romp, *A Willful Marriage*. And Anne Eames, who made her debut earlier in the year in Silhouette Desire's Celebration 1000, gives us more pleasure with *You're What?!* And if you enjoy a little melodrama with your romance, take a peek at Metsy Hingle's enthralling new book, *Backfire*.

As always, each and every Silhouette Desire is sensuous, emotional and sure to leave you feeling good at the end of the day!

Happy Reading!

Lucia Macro

Senior Editor

Please address questions and book requests to:
Silhouette Reader Service
U.S.: 3010 Walden Ave., P.O. Box 1325, Buffalo, NY 14269
Canadian: P.O. Box 609, Fort Erie, Ont. L2A 5X3

CAIT LONDON
TALLCHIEF'S BRIDE

SILHOUETTE *Desire*®
Published by Silhouette Books
America's Publisher of Contemporary Romance

If you purchased this book without a cover you should be aware that this book is stolen property. It was reported as "unsold and destroyed" to the publisher, and neither the author nor the publisher has received any payment for this "stripped book."

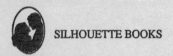

SILHOUETTE BOOKS

ISBN 0-373-76021-3

TALLCHIEF'S BRIDE

Copyright © 1996 by Lois Kleinsasser

All rights reserved. Except for use in any review, the reproduction or utilization of this work in whole or in part in any form by any electronic, mechanical or other means, now known or hereafter invented, including xerography, photocopying and recording, or in any information storage or retrieval system, is forbidden without the written permission of the editorial office, Silhouette Books, 300 East 42nd Street, New York, NY 10017 U.S.A.

All characters in this book have no existence outside the imagination of the author and have no relation whatsoever to anyone bearing the same name or names. They are not even distantly inspired by any individual known or unknown to the author, and all incidents are pure invention.

This edition published by arrangement with Harlequin Books S.A.

® and TM are trademarks of Harlequin Books S.A., used under license. Trademarks indicated with ® are registered in the United States Patent and Trademark Office, the Canadian Trade Marks Office and in other countries.

Printed in U.S.A.

Books by Cait London

Silhouette Desire

*The Loving Season #502
*Angel vs. MacLean #593
The Pendragon Virus #611
*The Daddy Candidate #641
†Midnight Rider #726
The Cowboy #763
Maybe No, Maybe Yes #782
†The Seduction of Jake Tallman #811
Fusion #871
The Bride Says No #891
Mr. Easy #919
Miracles and Mistletoe #968
‡The Cowboy and the Cradle #1006
‡Tallchief's Bride #1021

Silhouette Yours Truly

Every Girl's Guide To...
Every Groom's Guide To...

Silhouette Books

Spring Fancy 1994
   "Lightfoot and Loving"

*The MacLeans
†The Blaylocks
‡The Tallchiefs

CAIT LONDON

lives in the Missouri Ozarks but loves to travel the Northwest's gold rush/cattle drive trails every summer. She loves research trips, meeting people and going to Native American dances. Ms. London is an avid reader who loves to paint, play with computers and grow herbs (particularly scented geraniums right now). She's a national bestselling and award-winning author, and she also writes historical romance novels under another pseudonym. Three is her lucky number; she has three daughters, and the events in her life have always been in threes. "I love writing for Silhouette," she says. "One of the best perks about all this hard work is the thrilling reader response and the warm, snug sense that I have given readers an enjoyable, entertaining gift."

To Kerry and her Ava Gardner traits.

When a man of Fearghus blood places the ring upon the right woman's finger, he'll capture his true love forever.

What a mart ( ) a quiet ah his is the man
upon his upon fashion compute to Westlake
but the first Center

Prologue

Wyoming October winds whipped Tallchief Mountain; fear chilled seventeen-year-old Calum Tallchief. Duncan, his older brother by a year, and Fiona, his ten-year-old sister, were missing. With the experience of a mountain tracker, Calum listened to the night and pushed through the lashing pine boughs. The night clouds swept aside briefly, allowing him a glance at the white crests of the waves on Tallchief Lake. In a small, quiet meadow, high on the mountain, leaves tumbled across his parents' new graves.

The five Tallchiefs had just been orphaned. Matthew and Pauline Tallchief had stopped at a convenience store to buy a pizza for their children; they had interrupted a robbery in progress and been killed instantly.

Afterward, Calum had buried himself in his dad's small, tidy office, trying to make sense of the family's home and Tallchief Cattle Ranch accounts. Wrapped in grief, he had forgotten Fiona's desperate fear that her brothers and sister would be torn apart. As the youngest, she needed reassurance constantly.

Calum stopped, glanced at a herd of deer passing to a lower meadow, and heard Duncan's low, quiet voice, carried on the cold, unrelenting wind, and followed the sound. A branch cracked in the bush behind him, and Birk, Calum's younger brother by a year, spoke to Elspeth, just fourteen. She answered in the quiet, soothing tone that reminded Calum of his mother. He fought the tears burning his eyes and dashed them angrily away.

He had preferred the logic of numbers to a grieving ten-year-old sister, and had barricaded himself behind the safety of accounts. There was no logic in the murder of their parents. The circle was not complete. The unfinished cycle, that of his parents growing old and holding the grandchildren they wanted—

The wind passed through the trees on the mountain, and Calum remembered his father's gray eyes lighting with love as he looked at his wife. Matthew Tallchief's voice had come from his heart, the quiet, deep sound of a man's certainty. "Wait for the right woman, son. There's more than the body's fire between a man and a woman. And when the right woman comes along, she'll lead you on a merry chase, you with your numbers and plans and logic. You can't arrange love, son. It comes waltzing into your life when you least expect it. Turns things upside down, and things happen fast after that. Can't say it's all logic and roses. But it's worth every minute."

His parents had had more than enough love to keep their family warm and to give to others when it was needed. Then, with two shots, they had been ripped away.

Was he frightened for himself? Maybe. Was he frightened for the others? Yes.

"Calum, listen to your heart," his mother had said. How could he listen, when it was filled with grief and fear?

He moved into a small clearing near the lake to find Duncan holding Fiona up against him. Her pale legs dangled down his longer ones. She had been carefully wrapped against the cold in a thick quilt made by their mother. The wind whipped against them both, sending their black hair flying in the moonlight. When Duncan turned slowly to look at him, Calum saw the startling reflection of his raw anguish and fear in his brother's expression.

Calum moved close, blocking the wind and meeting Duncan's eyes, silver in the moonlight, over Fiona's head. They were men now; they had lost a portion of their boyhood when they tracked their parents' murderer. Calum remembered how, riding on horseback, the Tallchief brothers had tracked the murderer into the mountains. Only the Tallchiefs possessed the skill to track at night, and the sheriff had known it. Matthew Tallchief had taught his sons well, and at dawn they'd ridden back to Amen Flats. Bruised and shaking with fear, the murderer had cowered and walked behind their horses. He'd been glad to see the sheriff, running to his protection.

The three sons of Matthew and Pauline had nodded grimly to the sheriff and ridden away as men. They'd returned to the ranch, where Elspeth had been keeping Fiona safe.

Calum's heart tore as he read Duncan's fear and knew it for his own. It would be no easy feat to keep them all together and the mountain for their own.

Could they keep together?

Could they keep Tallchief Mountain and the ranch?

As the oldest, Duncan would try to do both. The mountain was their inheritance, the same as their gray eyes, given to them by Una Fearghus, a Scots bondwoman captured by Tallchief, a Sioux chieftain. In the end, she'd tamed him, and they'd settled upon the mountain; the rocky cliffs and lush meadows had reminded her of Scotland.

Calum blinked away his tears as he met Duncan's anguished stare. Calum swallowed and, to hide his fear and grief, muttered tightly, "So you've got her. You should have left a note."

Birk and Elspeth arrived, the wind slashing at their coal-black hair, an inheritance from their Sioux great-great-grandfather, Tallchief.

Then Duncan reached into the pitch-black night, lifted his hand into the cold wind and united them.

Later, Calum would think of that night as magic, when somehow Duncan managed to snag upon an idea. He added glue to the need to survive as a family, to keep their inheritance. "Aye!" they had shouted, raising their thumbs to the whirling tempest in the night sky. "Aye!"

Though it was no game to survive, alone and too young, the
five hurled forth their childhood names upon the cold wind—
Duncan the defender, Calum the cool, Birk the rogue, Elspeth
the elegant and Fiona the fiery.

They had a job to do—good grades, no trouble, each working to keep Tallchief Ranch.

The five Tallchiefs also pledged to return Una's lost dowry—
sold to keep Tallchief Mountain—to the family.

They would each seek and find one item of the dowry. A
ring with three garnets held in a Celtic design fell to Calum.

He promised the others and himself that he would find it.
Because the seasons had to have meaning, and the circles had
to be completed.

One

"**Y**ou'd like me to find whoever is sabotaging Unique. Is that correct?" Calum Tallchief interrupted the frustrating man. Seated in front of Unique Import-Export's chairman of the board, Calum preferred to slice through chitchat; he wanted to finish this assignment quickly, all the ends neatly tied. Then he wanted to find a family heirloom that had been included in his great-great-grandmother's dowry. Calum wanted the Tallchief heirloom returned to his family.

Calum Tallchief was very good at tying loose ends. He kept his life neatly packaged, and soon he would have the ring. It had been traced to Denver, which stretched out and glistened in the morning sun beyond the executive office.

The son of a mountain tracker and the descendant of a Sioux chieftain, Calum did not trust the uneasiness that ran up the back of his neck. Maybe it was because all Tallchiefs got restless in October, the month when their parents had been killed and when their stormy emotions rode near the surface.

Emotions? Calum kept his tightly wrapped, except when in the midst of his family. The ring had not been important in his

life, though he had given his pledge long ago, when the five
Tallchiefs, newly orphaned, had raised their hands to the night
sky and shouted, "Aye!"

He'd been too busy surviving to claim the ring. Calum inhaled slightly. Just like his marriage, the ring represented unfinished business.

Roger Olson, chairman of Unique's board, lightly touched
his hair and his bald spots. The early-October sunshine
drenching Denver's streets skimmed through the office window to gleam on his head and on the hand mirror he'd been
using. "Before someone put hair remover in my styling gel, I
had a head of hair, too. Even my private washroom isn't safe.
It's a case of business *and* personal sabotage, Tallchief. That's
why I hired you to find whoever is doing this and protect me."

Calum glanced at the washroom door. Anyone could have
picked the lock. Fiona, his youngest sister, could do it behind
her back in one second flat.

He rolled his shoulder within his gray suit jacket. His six-
foot-four-inch body resented the long drive to Denver from his
home in Amen Flats, Wyoming.

The stone that had been Tallchief's nestled warmly against
Calum's chest. Worn smooth with age and bound by a leather
thong, the stone had been given to Calum by his father. Matthew Tallchief had known when he met his life's mate, Calum's mother; he had given her the stone, an obsidian, in a
tradition that had begun with the first Tallchief and was now
passed on to Calum. For a time, Calum had set aside the stone
as he built his career. October and the search for the ring
seemed good reasons to wear Tallchief's mark. Roger Olson
continued to drone, and Calum shifted restlessly. "If someone is sabotaging Unique, Inc., there will be a trail. I'll find
it," Calum stated.

"You're the best corporate hit man in the area—" Olson
began, then noted Calum's quiet, cool look. "Okay, okay,
you're supposed to be a top-notch corporate investigator. I just
want this mess cleaned up and fast."

Olson glanced at Calum's glasses, then down the length of
his expensive tie and across his broad shoulders, clad in the
light gray suit jacket. His envious gaze rose to Calum's neatly

clipped straight black hair, another inheritance from his great-great-grandfather, Tallchief.

Olson preened in the mirror, a fiftyish man trying to look thirty. "I'm a researcher, too, a pretty good one. I checked you out."

"Did you?" Calum asked slowly.

Olson didn't recognize the cool invitation of a professional, used to getting information and giving none. "You're a cool one, Tallchief. You're thirty-six and widowed. You've got an older brother, Duncan, who's got a ranch on Tallchief Mountain—he's done some work finding kidnapped children—and you have a younger brother and two sisters. You live in Amen Flats, Wyoming, a wide spot in the road. You're part Scots—guess that's where you get those cold gray eyes from—and part Sioux...guess that's where you get that black hair and your dark coloring. You come highly recommended by the firms you listed in your résumé."

Again he glanced down Calum's tall, lean body, then sucked in his belly. He eased his suit jacket over his stomach. "You don't talk much, but I'm pretty good at selecting people."

Calum nodded and noticed Olson's eyes cutting to his secretary, who had quietly entered the office. The woman, dressed in a navy blue suit with a long skirt and practical pumps, passed through the room to place a stack of papers on the desk. A pencil was thrust through the dowdy, tidy knot of hair on top of her head, and she wore no makeup behind large glasses. Her cheekbones were high, probably a Slavic inheritance, and matched the angle of her mouth, set in a firm jaw. A streak of gray ran from her temple into the severe knot. Olson's expression dripped with lust, his stare locked on her prim, buttoned-to-the-throat white blouse. He showed his teeth in a leer before the woman nodded and turned to leave.

Calum noted her ears, and the tiny holes of missing earrings. Her glasses were probably purchased from a discount rack, and the lenses struck him as nonprescription glass. Her suit was modest and inexpensive.

Olson's gaze dropped to the woman's ample backside, lost within the folds of her loose jacket, and skimmed down her legs.

Calum noted that her legs were shapely, and too thin in proportion to her hips. The woman exited the room without a sound, the door closing behind her and leaving a delicate scent of jasmine.

Olson released the air he had been holding, since he'd sucked in his stomach. He glanced at Calum and leaned forward on his desk. "My secretary. Excellent work. Quiet, efficient. Knows how to keep her mouth shut ... Two to one she's a virgin. Takes a bit to get them to come around, if you know what I mean. I'm in the mood for a virgin, and I've been checking her over. I'll bet she's real hot. The quiet ones always are. I like a woman with big hips."

When Calum continued to look at him, Olson flinched. "Now get this, Tallchief. A man has a right to ... you know what I mean, play a bit on the side. This sabotage business is overlapping into my private life. I don't want my wife to know. It could be real messy if she or her old man found out I was getting a little excitement once in a while." Olson jabbed a finger at the portrait of the man behind his desk. "I've been keeping this mess secret. That old man would kick me out in a minute if he knew I couldn't handle this. So it's just best if my wife or the old man doesn't know about your function here."

Calum listened to the slight rustling of paper coming from the intercom. He reached over to click it off, unnoticed by Olson. The man was sloppy about business and his relationships.

The older man smoothed the missing patches of his hair. "Play ball with me on this, Tallchief, and I'll see that you get all the business you can handle."

Calum inhaled slowly. He had more than enough work. He'd picked this offer from a stack of others because he wanted to look for the legendary Tallchief ring, which his sister Elspeth had traced to Denver.

His great-great-grandmother Una's dowry had been sold to keep Tallchief land. Calum's older brother, Duncan, had recently placed a Tallchief baby in the cradle he'd vowed to reclaim.

Was it October or four-month-old Megan that had started the restlessness within Calum? Or was it the challenge of his older brother's keeping his part of the promise to reclaim Una's dowry? Whatever the reason, Calum's tracker's instincts told him it was time to find the ring.

While Olson droned on, Calum automatically noted incidents he wanted to check out, yet his mind was on the ring. He supposed he had inherited the tendencies of all Tallchief males to keep what they considered theirs. He wondered whimsically whether he should have found the ring a long time ago to place on his wife's finger, then pushed the thought away. He preferred clean logic to the clutter of legends and whimsy. Sherry had died in a car accident five years ago; he'd never know whether the ring could have made their marriage strong.

While Olson continued to drone on, Calum listened on a professional level. On another level, he considered the success of his quest for the ring and his family. Elspeth, as keeper of Una's journals, and Sybil, Duncan's wife, were a good team. Sybil's occupation was recovering antiques and working in genealogy. She had helped Elspeth track the ring. Both women were graceful, cool, and powerful when set upon their course.

Sybil's purpose seemed at times to be focused on distracting Duncan and tormenting him into a smile, which she could do easily. Duncan, Sybil and Sybil's daughter, Emily, had bonded for life, and Megan had only added more joy.

Megan. Calum loved to hold and cuddle her. He tensed and shifted restlessly. It was true—October unleashed the Tallchiefs' emotions.

Olson's voice cut into Calum's thoughts. "I pride myself on picking the right man. Under that classy look, you've got an Indian look, Tallchief. A tough, cold look that would go a long way if you caught someone in a dark alley. Or draw good-looking women—" His eyes brightened, and he asked hopefully, "Say, how about if you and I go to a night spot tonight and relax a bit? I know you don't have a wife to account to."

"I have plans. Some other time?" Calum didn't like anyone rummaging through his private life, and he didn't want to socialize with Olson. He wanted to prowl through Unique's vacated offices after business hours.

The secretary entered the room again, moving just as quietly as before. Calum noted the slight slope of her shoulders, sometimes typical of office workers. He stood slowly, as Tallchief men were taught to do when a woman entered the room. Olson, taking the hint, leaped to his feet. He placed his hand with familiarity on the secretary's shoulder, clearly oblivious of her body's distinct recoil. "This is my secretary, Talia Smith. Talia, this is Calum Tallchief. Mr. Tallchief is serving as an advisor on one of my pilot projects. You'll probably see him poking into things. Help him if there is anything he needs."

"It's nice to meet you, Mr. Tallchief," the woman said very properly, in a low, well-modulated voice that bore a slight Texas twang.

Talia pasted a tight, pleasant smile on her face. Calum Tallchief had trouble written all over him. From what she had heard before the intercom was switched off, Olson had hired an expensive bird dog to check out the problems at Unique. Unlike Olson, Tallchief spoke little, asking precise questions in an even-toned voice.

He probably never shouted. Talia, who had grown up in a passionate, demonstrative and loving home, did not trust quiet men.

Calum had uncoiled himself from the chair with the grace of an athlete. The sunlight coming from the large windows glinted off his stylish glasses. The light slid in a blue sheen across his black hair and shone on his high cheekbones and hollowed, lean cheeks. Dressed in an expensive suit, Calum Tallchief reminded her of a steel stiletto, lean and deadly.

She chanced a brief, pointed look behind his glasses and found narrowed smoke-colored eyes framed by jet-black lashes. There was nothing comforting in the hard set of his jaw, or in the line of his mouth.

Beneath the suit jacket, he wore a pocket protector, just like every other corporate nerd she'd known. Nerds could be dangerous. Corporate nerds had brains that clicked like calculator buttons. This one looked as if he hadn't seen fun since time began.

Calum Tallchief towered over her five-foot-eight-inch—with heels—height. Her eyes were level with his expansive, Armani-clad chest. The gray-and-blue-striped tie was too perfect. Beneath Olson's overpowering cologne, Calum's scents of soap and a lime-scented after-shave were masculine and to the point.

To the point, Talia repeated mentally. This man did everything methodically and for a reason. Calum inclined his head and extended his hand to her for a handshake. "Ms. Smith."

His voice was deep and cool, making her think of danger just beneath the surface. He reminded her of a deep, quiet pool that she'd dived into from a rocky Acapulco cliff. The currents running beneath the gentle waves had almost drowned her. Talia stared at that large, tanned hand, with its neatly clipped nails. Hair slightly flecked the back. The hair at her nape lifted slightly as she slowly took his hand.

His fingers enfolded hers in a firm handshake that was soon gone. A layer of calluses lay in his broad palm. His eyes lingered, studying her closely. His gaze took in her glasses, purchased to disguise her long lashes and eyes, then slid from her left eye to her right one, their blue color concealed by tinted brown contact lenses.

Great. All she needed was a supersharp iceman, a corporate hit man, from the sound of it before the intercom clicked off. She'd listened to Olson's every conversation, and he'd never noticed, until today. Very likely it was Calum Tallchief who had noticed, not Olson.

Mentally she spit out a word in Swahili which translated as *elephant dung.*

Talia nodded, forcing her expression to be bland. "Do you need anything from me, Mr. Olson?"

"Not now, honey. Maybe later," he added with a meaningful leer that she let slide off her. She'd put up with his leers for months while she quietly destroyed him. Then she remembered that she was shy, dowdy Talia Smith and feigned a quiver, looking down at the floor. In the four months she had been working for Olson, it had taken every ounce of her will-power not to attack him. He'd go down in a soft flow of blubber, probably a whiner....

Talia felt Calum's stare on her back as she left the room in her practiced sloped-shoulder walk. Once in the outer area, her cubicle, Talia allowed her aching shoulders to straighten. She briefly rubbed the binding across her full breasts, relieving the uncomfortable pressure. She glanced in the mirror and checked the color on her hair. None of her naturally pale blond roots were showing. She'd achieved the dowdy brown color perfectly. She touched the gray hair extension she had added at her temple; it held firm.

She blinked her eyes—she was getting used to the tinted contact lenses. The fake, slightly hairy mole remained firmly pasted to her throat.

Talia stalked to a file drawer and jerked it open. Just great. Things had been perking along just fine until Olson finally showed a single dram of intelligence and hired an investigator. Talia muttered the Swahili word for elephant dung again. She flipped through the report she'd done on Calum Tallchief for Olson. Tallchief was a numbers genius, a widower, good references, resided in Amen Flats, Wyoming...brothers, sisters... Worked his way through college while helping raise his younger brother, Birk, and the two sisters, Elspeth and Fiona. Part owner of Tallchief Cattle Ranch, managed by brother Duncan. Respected family. An office in his home in Amen Flats, managed family investments. No record of— Talia snapped the file shut. In her two-week stint as a detective's assistant, she'd discovered how to identify a doctored background check. Calum Tallchief had supplied little but a list of references that Olson had apparently checked out.

Talia tapped the file with her short, neat nails. She glanced at them, a part of her disguise. She couldn't wait for revenge and for long, red-hot nails. Until then, she wanted to prove that Olson would pant after a woman who didn't wear short skirts or figure-revealing clothing. She would give him no cause to think she was available.

For four long months, she had been slaving for Olson, carefully plotting how to destroy him.

Seven months ago, Olson had sexually harassed Talia's sister. Jan, a sweet young housewife who badly needed a job, hadn't known how to handle Olson's unwanted attention. Within three months from when he hired Jan as his executive secretary, Olson had destroyed her life. Jan had been afraid to tell her husband about Olson's blatant pursuit. Eventually, Jan's husband had come to believe she'd taken a lover; Roy had walked out. Jan had been shattered and had returned to the Petrovna family home in Texas. Roy remained inconsolable in Denver.

Talia's father, Michael Petrovna, part Russian and part Apache, wanted to kill him, or at the least tie him down on an anthill and pour honey over his "overactive parts." Her brother, Alek, a tough newspaper correspondent, wanted to slaughter Olson, first in the news and then in an isolated alley. Anton, another brother and a business genius, wanted to bankrupt Olson. Talia, just in from surfing in Hawaii, had barely managed to convince the three Petrovna males to let her do the job. She believed a slow disintegration from the inside of Olson's business was the best revenge. She wanted to drive him so low that he would contact Roy, admitting his deeds. Talia was experienced in creating chaos. It was her unique talent.

Talia placed a glass against the door and listened to Olson drone and to Calum's quiet, short questions. She didn't trust a man who spoke little and looked too much. Calum Tallchief had noted her missing earrings.

She would wear tiny pearl studs the next day, a neat recovery. Olson would probably take that as a come-on, and that was unfortunate. She wanted him to come all the way, to box himself in so perfectly that there could be no mistake about who was chasing whom. Talia shook her head and moved away from the door, just as Calum Tallchief opened it.

His cool glance slid to her, then to the glass on her desk. Great. This guy might put two and two together, something Olson was incapable of—even after she'd she planted a computer virus in his accounts-tracking system.

Talia hunched her shoulders and slid into her desk chair. She placed the earphones on her head and began transcribing another boring, overworded threatening letter from Olson to a client. Then she caught Calum's fresh-soap-and-male scent and inhaled. Just what she needed, a professional, oversize, cool corporate bird dog nerd. There probably wasn't a thing running around in his brain but numbers.

Olson came into her cubicle, and she decided to let the giant magnet in her purse stay there. Drifting it over the computer tapes that held the company's entire resources of customers would have to wait for another time. The magnet would wipe out the tapes, and restoring the information base would take months of costly marketing time.

Olson's meaty hand weighted her shoulder. He bent close to her ear to whisper, "Be nice to the guy, honey. Take him around, show him what he wants."

"Yes, sir," she returned, neatly stacking her work and rising to her feet. Her artificially padded hips bumped the desk. Talia readjusted them with a rubbing motion of her hand.

Calum Tallchief opened the office door for her. He continued to open doors for her. He must have learned that in Nerd Basics. She introduced him to the heads of the departments, waited while they briefed him on schedules and procedures, and then took him to the next department. The man she was baby-sitting drew women's eyes like magnets.

By the end of the day, Talia had decided that Calum had the mental tenacity of a bulldog. If she avoided a question, he managed to circle back to it. A regular listmaker, with all the checks in place. At quitting time he'd had the building's plans spread on the conference table. He'd looked just as immaculate as when the day began, as though he had been dipped in cool plastic. She'd watched him methodically track air vents and heating systems. Darn. Just when she had figured out how to eject a stink bomb every time Olson flushed his private toilet.

Then there was that nasty business of demanding that Sleazeball toss away all of the toiletries in his private washroom. Her neat dusting of itch powder on the toilet paper roll had been foiled when Calum requested a new one.

Anyone who had a high-security lock for the washroom within one hour couldn't be trusted to think normally. Any nerd with calluses on his palm was not normal.

Calum Tallchief wasn't ruining her plans for Mr. Sleazeball. Too bad that all that gorgeous, neatly clipped jet-black hair might start falling out the next time he combed his hair. At just the right, critical moment, she'd manage to drop in a tidbit about an article she'd read: It was true that in certain stress environments, baldness was catching. He needed to go elsewhere, because she intended to create a stress-mountain.

Talia smiled tightly. She'd never destroyed a nerd before, but if she had to disassemble Calum Tallchief to get to Olson, she would. In her experience, nerds went haywire when something unexplainable got tossed into their path. She'd just have to find that certain something.

From the conference room, Calum watched Talia and the other employees get onto the city bus. He glanced quickly at her personnel file and found it too clean. Then he moved quickly into her cubicle and sat at her desk. A secretary usually knew more than anyone, and she had access to Olson's washroom. It was a start. A quick search revealed nothing, except that the desk was too neat.

Too neat worried him. He stashed away that fact and turned on her computer. It was linked in the system, as was everyone else's. He inserted a disk that would automatically try a series of access codes that she might use. *Jerk* popped up right after *Jane.* Calum pushed everything else from his mind and dusted her computer for fingerprints. He lifted a good set, made a few calls to technicians who would work off-hours. He flipped through her personnel file, noted that she was approaching forty, had never been married and had recently moved from Baltimore; Maryland was supposedly her native state. Calum tapped the form just once; Miss Smith was definitely a Texan. Then he began prowling through her computer.

In the morning, Calum opened the door for Talia as she entered. Today she was wearing tiny pearl studs and a shapeless dark dress with a tiny rosebud print. "Good morning, Mr. Tallchief," she said pleasantly as she slid her large, unfash-

ionable purse into a drawer. Calum wondered just what was in
that bag. Talia Smith played an exciting game, though she did
not look it. A new employee, she had quickly learned how to
infiltrate the computer system. One huge list of clients had
been tampered with, the addresses all the same—"Blue Moon
Road."

She opened her desk drawer and searched the contents, and
her expression chilled momentarily. Then she smiled at him,
her eyes skipping down his taupe suit. "You're here early."

He sat on the chair opposite her and noted the grim line of
her untinted lips. Calum tossed her something to chew on. "I
slept here."

The tiniest bit of anger flashed in her obviously tinted contact lenses. "Really? Couldn't you find accommodations? I'll
be happy to find you a room, if you wish."

"Thank you, but I'm comfortable here."

"I see," Talia said, her voice clipped. She began briskly or-
ganizing her desk for the day. In a few moments, she noticed
that he hadn't moved. She peered over the top of her glasses.
"May I help you find anything, Mr. Tallchief?"

The polite nudge to get him out of her way didn't work.
Calum traced the small, firm line appearing between her dark
brows. He hoped he was interrupting her schedule for sabotage. He also noted that the tracker within him was stirring.
"I'm waiting for Olson."

"He should be here at any moment. I have to make coffee
in his office. He likes it to be ready when he arrives. Would you
like a cup?"

"Yes. Thank you." He rose to follow her into Olson's office. "Do you always make coffee for him in the morning?"

"Yes. Always. He likes his desk tidied and the blinds opened
and a sweet roll waiting for him. Excuse me." She left to return with a large, nutty sweet roll and placed it on the expansive desk. "I'm sorry. I only bought one. Would you like
something?"

"No, thank you." He'd noted the sweet roll she had hidden
beneath a napkin. The scent of coffee wafted through the
room, and he longed for the fresh, clean mountain air of
Amen Flats. Calum thought of Elspeth's freshly baked bread

and berry jam. A sweet ache shot through him. The Tall-chiefs were a close family, bonded by love and hard times.

Duncan had been the first of the Tallchiefs to prove the truth of a Tallchief legend—*When a woman brings the cradle to a man of Fearghus blood, she will fill it with his babies.* To their marriage, Sybil had brought Emily, a teenage daughter the Tallchief family adored. Then gray-eyed, black-haired Megan, with her baby scents—

He wondered briefly what mischief his brother Birk and Lacey MacCandliss were up to, battling away at each other. The Tallchiefs had unofficially adopted Lacey. Her child-hood had been abusive, and though the rest of the Tallchiefs adored Lacey, she'd never ceased to be the thorn in Birk's life-style.

Duncan would be wallowing in the love he had waited for, had deserved for years. Sybil would be putting Megan, their baby, down to nap. She would start her work then, hunting for family history or maybe a lost antique. Sybil's nemesis, Mar-cella Portway, wanted Sybil to find a royal Spanish gene in her family tree, and she refused to be dislodged from Sybil's cli-entele.

Elspeth would be at her loom—one that Tallchief had made for Una—her home serene and filled with the scent of herbs and freshly baked bread. Calum frowned. Elspeth worried him. As a girl, she and her mother had worked on Una's jour-nals, and now Elspeth spoke little of her quest—the paisley shawl. Once she'd been excited about the Tallchiefs' legends and suddenly, after a visit to Scotland, Elspeth did not speak of the shawl.

Then there was Fiona, the youngest Tallchief and a rebel down to her bones. Perhaps that was because as a teenager she had had to strain to be very good in the older Tallchiefs' keeping. One wrong move, and the authorities would have been ready to claim her. Fiona had found ways to take out her moods on the family, if not the world. Now that she was grown, if there was a cause—human or animal rights, pollu-tion or government injustice—Fiona would be in the midst of it. Calum hadn't received a notice to bail her out of jail lately, but he expected her call at any time. Things were too quiet in Montana, the location of Fiona's present project.

Then Calum turned his mind to the job he had taken and watched Talia Smith prepare the office for Olson.

Olson steamed into the room minutes later, curses heating the air around him. He slammed an invoice on the desk with one hand and a bouquet of flowers with the other. "I'll find who's responsible for this, and when I do— Some jerk has doubled our order for frozen Swedish herrings and had them shipped to a holding warehouse in Africa. That was no typing error. We're just building that market, and they'll have to be gone before their shelf life runs out. We'll have to sell cut-rate. *If* they are still frozen."

He plopped into his chair, took a big bite of sweet roll, munched on it and thrust the bouquet at Talia. "Here, honey. There's a present on your desk," he muttered, glaring at Calum. "What have you found?"

Then Olson scowled at Talia as she was leaving. "I tried to call you last night. I thought we might do some work at your place—or the corporate apartment. Where were you?"

Clearly dismayed, Talia's hand rose to her cheek as she turned to him. "Oh, dear. I'm so sorry. I must have fallen asleep early."

Olson scowled at her briefly. "Yeah, well...okay. But if you want to go up in Unique, you've got to play ball, got it?"

She nodded demurely. "Yes, sir. I understand that it is sometimes necessary to work at odd hours."

"Now you've got it, honey. Why don't you run along and open your present?"

When Olson demanded results, Calum reported finding the "Blue Moon Road" addresses and that he had restored the proper ones. The older man patted the too-curly wig he had adopted and looked nervous when it slipped. He punched the intercom, and Talia responded in a professional tone. Olson muttered, "Anything Tallchief wants, you do. Okay? Did you like the present?"

There was a pause, and then Talia said very quietly, "Thank you for the Hot Nights and Passion perfume. But I couldn't possibly accept such a gift. A bottle this size is terribly expensive, isn't it?''

"Baby, you're worth it." Olson leered and preened at the same time. He picked up his hand mirror, lifted the toupee, glanced at his missing hair and scowled. Without clicking off the intercom, he glanced at Calum. "Just a matter of time, Tallchief, and I'll nail her."

Calum turned off the intercom. He decided not to mention the potential of a sexual harassment suit. No one had brought charges against Olson, though office gossip had insinuated that he had been very busy. A scan through the personnel files showed a high percentage of women who had entered and then left the company. Motives for revenge against Olson wouldn't be hard to find.

"I don't think this will take long," Calum murmured. Meanwhile, he decided to keep Talia's mind and fingers busy.

Calum walked into Talia's cubicle to find her stuffing an opulent perfume bottle into a drawer. "Mr. Olson is always so generous," she murmured.

"How do you feel about that?" Calum asked, noting an assortment of other gifts in the drawer.

"I wouldn't want to hurt his feelings by refusing him. I need this job," she said softly. She sniffed, and he noted the teardrop hovering on her lashes.

He was a sucker for tears and sniffs, though the world didn't know it. It was in his Tallchief genes, and his sisters knew it well. From the look of her, Talia Smith was probably sheltered and couldn't picture being roughly used on Olson's desk. "Would you mind calling this list of pawnshop and antique shops and asking about a garnet ring? Here's a drawing to help you describe it," he said, placing Elspeth's drawing on the desk.

Her lashes fluttered, and she looked down, the perfect picture of a victim. Her shoulders slumped, and she sniffed once more. Calum fought to keep his protective tendencies under control. He decided grimly that Olson wasn't going to destroy another innocent woman, not even one who was disrupting the company. Then Talia murmured, "It looks beautiful. I'll try very hard to find it. Mr. Olson said to accommodate you."

Calum inhaled sharply. He disliked Olson's sexual harass-ment of his female employees. Her tone implied that Olson wanted her to share sexual favors with Calum. Though it had been some time since his wife had died in the accident, Tall-chiefs weren't sexual butterflies. Talia made him feel like a heel for associating with Olson.

He found himself reasoning that perhaps she had had a valid reason for having Olson sign a document changing the com-pany's health policy. Female employees were now allowed to stay home with sick infants. Calum doubted that Olson had known what he was signing, or that the policy had taken ef-fect. His signature was also on a huge order for unmarketable artwork. While bits of trails led to Talia's desk, she didn't de-serve being cornered by Olson. "It's a family ring," he ex-plained too sharply. "I would appreciate your efforts, but only if you have time and it doesn't interfere with your profes-sional standards."

Calum left her office with a feeling that he was going to pay dearly for not turning Talia Smith over to Olson. He'd pro-tected his sisters all his life, and he suspected that Talia was benefiting from the Tallchief traditional respect of women.

Over the next three days, Calum noted and was disgusted by Olson's obvious pursuit of the unattainable Talia. Her boss never missed a chance to stroke her arm, and his gaze on her ample hips dripped with lust. The day he followed her into the copier room, Calum was on the point of entering to protect her. Within minutes, Talia exited the room, an untidy stack of papers in her hand, her face flushed and her blouse loosened. She glared at Calum and puffed by him, her wide hips swing-ing. Olson opened the door, drew his jacket over the huge inkstain on his belly and smiled curtly. "Just a little accident. Come into my office. I've got problems."

Calum followed, remembering Talia's furious expression. He didn't blame her for cooling down her boss.

Olson shut his office door. "You're good, Tallchief. But I have to tell you that someone knows where the company apartment is, and they are playing with me. Last night I was there...uh, you know...entertaining on company busi-ness...when the fax rang. Now, here I am, getting mellow with a red-hot— Uh...I was working hard. Here comes this fax that says, *Bozo, hanky-panky isn't company business. What would Daddy think?* That's all I need, someone turning me in to my father-in-law. I want this jerk out of my life. Do something!''

Calum studied the fax. The words had been clipped out and pasted on, and the message sent from a commercial service. The clue wasn't worth tracing; the sender had probably used an alias and a disguise. He almost admired the sender. Almost.

Two

That night, Calum leaned back into the shadows of the alley. Seventeen stories up, Olson was scheduled for an after-hours massage in Unique's corporate apartment. The exclusive penthouse could only be accessed by a security key. Olson had the only key to the new lock, suggested by Calum.

Calum caught the scent of the trees planted in the concrete sidewalks and a drift of cold, crisp night air. Above the street lamps, the stars twinkled just as they would over Tallchief Mountain.

Calum traced a woman walking briskly down the street. She reminded him of his wife—tall, black hair and white skin, efficient, business written all over her, carrying a briefcase. As a sensuous woman, Sherry had liked men to admire her, in business and in private. For a time, the marriage had purred along smoothly, carefully planned by both of them. Yet just months after their marriage, small arguments, distasteful to them both, had arisen like a bed of nettles. A beautiful woman, Sherry had viewed marriage as a shield from which to test her flirtations. Though Calum missed the long, hot nights in her arms, he didn't miss the jealousy that she could easily ignite. He wondered briefly whether he shouldn't have looked away when Sherry played her femme fatale role, enticing men to her like bees to honey.

They'd never been friends; lust hadn't allowed the time. Sherry had been his first strong attraction; they'd wanted each other immediately. They'd both been up-and-coming executives. Marriage had seemed logical to them both, and the heat had continued for several months into their marriage.

When his jealousy first began, Calum hadn't liked the dark side of himself.

Sherry had wanted an upscale corporate life. She had come into his life a sexually experienced woman, and he'd found himself looking at her old lovers when they socialized. Maybe he should have been more— Sherry's car had slammed into a truck just after a flaming argument. Calum would carry that guilt with him for an eternity.

He'd run that argument through his mind a thousand times. Sherry had wanted to "cultivate" a potential investor at a private dinner with him. When Calum ordered her to stay home, she'd tossed at him everything she hated about their lives—and no, she wouldn't live in Amen Flats . . . ever. . . .

She never had.

Perhaps his expectations had been too high. Calum had expected his parents' deep love to develop in his own marriage. Matthew and Pauline's marriage had been ideal, their lives bonded by love, children and the land. Duncan had found that love with Sybil.

Visits to Duncan's warm, busy home emphasized the stark emptiness of Calum's life. Perhaps that was why at times he preferred to stay away from Amen Flats or to lurk in his sterile modern home.

He adjusted his collar against the cold night air. At thirty-six, he was likely experiencing a nesting urge, a biological need to produce another Tallchief baby. Calum exhaled sharply. He'd wrapped himself in computers and his profession, a neatly crafted, logically safe lair in which to brood alone. Lately he had been feeling the loneliness of his life. And his bed, to be honest. His body was protesting abstinence, and his life seemed uninteresting.

He liked routine, neatness and logic. There was no reason Talia Smith's little tricks should excite him even slightly. Yet he had enjoyed strolling through her computer gambits and unraveling them.

Calum's eyes narrowed against the glare of streetlights as he traced a figure moving swiftly toward the building. His mind lingered a moment on the past, the warmth of a woman moving in his arms, under him. The scent of lovemaking— Maybe he'd wanted too much from Sherry, a beautiful woman who loved the admiration of all men. Maybe he was still half in love with her. Because the memory of their lovemaking haunted him. That was why he preferred sleeping on Unique's boardroom couch, rather than in an empty bed—when he could sleep at all.

After his computer screen was turned off and the business deals completed, reality painted his life in cold, empty colors. Though he loved his family, there was a big, illogical hole inside him. Only investigating financial packages or firms, or tracking down a corporate mischiefmaker like Olson's, eased whatever drove him.

Guilt? If their marriage had lasted longer than those few months, would it have survived? Maybe he wasn't cut out for the warmth of a relationship, though he had tried.

He shifted restlessly, pushing his hands into the pockets of his black leather jacket. Nights of sleeping in Unique's conference room had aggravated an old rodeo injury, a rib long healed. Back then, the Tallchiefs had badly needed the money to survive as a family.

A slender boy dressed in the apartment building's valet uniform entered the well-lit foyer. He nodded to the watchman, showed his identity badge. Calum leaned against the brick wall and noted the lights dimming in Unique's suite. He went back to waiting with the patience that had earned him a reputation. Suddenly, a motion above him caught his eye.

A window opened; a black boot, followed by slender legs and a body stepped out onto a narrow ledge that ran beneath the penthouse. Calum moved quickly, taking the elevator to the fifteenth floor and quietly entering the hallway. It was two more floors up to Olson's penthouse. Calum listened at a suspect apartment door for a moment, then deftly picked the lock and entered.

The valet jacket was tossed over a chair. From the open window, Calum saw the intruder angle around a corner and begin edging upward. He threw a grappling hook and began to climb.

Calum stepped out onto the narrow ledge. Whoever was scaling the building knew what he was doing. Using a rope and scaling hooks, the slender man was dressed in black and wore a black cap. He wore a mountain climber's safety belt, which was attached to the rope. He swung out from the building, expertly bounced his feet against it and swung around the corner. Calum inched his way to a safety ladder and then to the dangling rope.

The intruder was now on the ledge near the penthouse and extracting something from the bag at his waist. Calum took a deep breath, tested the rope and pushed away from the building. He swung around the corner, landed neatly on another narrow ledge and looked into the blackened face of a startled boy.

The boy muttered something that sounded like an African curse with a Texas twang.

Calum noted the black glove gripping the windowsill; the boy's other hand held a camera rigged for night shots. "Hello. Having fun?" Calum asked pleasantly.

The boy jammed the camera into a bag at his waist and began inching backward on the narrow ledge.

"Let's make this easy," Calum began, dismissing a woman's high giggle within the apartment. "You come down with me and I'll see that the charges are less than what they should be."

He didn't like the curt tone of the intruder's curse. "Be reasonable. You could get killed. Blackmail isn't worth it," he said slowly, fighting his rising temper.

The youth was agile, leaping to another ledge and flattening himself against the wall. Calum glanced downward, took another breath and followed. He never lost his temper, but working with Olson hadn't helped his mood.

Calum sucked in his breath as the youth missed a step, angled for a foothold and began searching for an escape. Calum didn't want to panic the boy; it could be fatal. When he was young, Calum had had a few antics of his own, and his good luck had held. The boy's luck might not. Calum talked quietly. "There isn't any way out. I've got you. Take it easy and you'll be safe."

The youth reached upward to grasp a window ledge, and Calum noted the high line of a woman's bosom and the neat curve of a firm bottom, running into long legs that ended in black boots. Her cap slipped off, tumbling down into the night's abyss. A long, smooth swath of hair unfurled and ran down her back.

She glared at him, her eyes glittering within the black face paint. "Would you mind getting off my ledge? In case you haven't noticed, it's occupied." Her tone was proper and indignant.

His hand shot out to grip her wrist. She released her grip on the ledge, and they overbalanced. Calum grabbed the ledge and drew her closer at the same time, steadying them. He looked down into Talia's furious expression.

Despite a precarious position seventeen stories above the street, Calum found the situation amusing. He glanced down her trim, athletic body and fought the immediate jerk of his awakening body. "Did you forget your hips, Miss Smith?"

"Stop leering. You look like Olson," she snapped, trying to pull her wrist away. Her skin was warm and supple, smooth and soft, beneath his fingers.

"I'm not exactly happy," he muttered. Seventeen stories above the ground, a mayhem-causing female smelling of jasmine had just alerted his deprived sexual needs.

Olson's voice sounded inside the penthouse. "Come to Daddy, Little Red Riding Hood." Calum glanced into the window and saw Olson's bare backside running into another room. He was following a blonde dressed in a red bonnet and scanty lace briefs.

Talia watched the blonde's flight. "She could use a work-out program and less heavy sauces in her diet."

Calum sought and found a latch. He picked the latch and opened the window. "You seem experienced. Maybe I should let you do this. Get in."

Her eyes widened briefly and narrowed. "Look, guy. You can't just pick me up on a ledge and then start telling me what—"

He pushed her into the room.

"I've got plans for the evening, big boy. Sorry," she said lightly, and turned. "Some other time."

Calum caught the back of her climbing belt before she took the first step away from him. Olson's giggle sounded, closer now, and Calum jerked open a closet door and pushed his captive into it.

"Just what do you think you're doing—?" she began before he placed his hand over her mouth.

While he was checking out the dark linen closet, she bit him, hard. Calum tensed, pushed his face down to hers, and between his teeth, said very softly and distinctly, "Shut up. Or I'll open this door and explain your little plan to destroy Olson."

"Nerd," she muttered after a full second of debate passed through her narrowed eyes. "Stop crowding me, you jerk. You're taking up all the space and all the air. You know that sleazeball deserves a good dose of blackmail."

"Lady, you need to be taught some manners, and there is a stiff penalty for blackmail." Calum rubbed his injured hand and tried not to think about the soft flow of her body bumping against his. When she squirmed, he locked his hand on her climbing belt and jerked slightly. "You're not going anywhere."

She straightened, and the top of her head butted his chin. The movement knocked his head against a shelf and caused his glasses to bump painfully against his nose. Her slight satisfied smile told him that Talia Smith deliberately created accidents to suit her.

Olson's call entered the dark closet. "Come to Wolfie, my little feastable."

"Ohh, my big strong daddy..." the blonde cooed.

Talia's boot heel stood on Calum's toe, and he wrapped both arms around her from the back and lifted her off the floor. "You put me down, you big bozo!"

"Bozo," he repeated. "I bet you had a hard time finding that word to cut out for your fax pasting job."

The feminine bottom squirming agilely against his lower belly caused Calum to go very still. His body reacted irrationally to Talia's. This was the wrong woman, and the wrong time to be distracted. In a hushed whisper, he spoke into her ear. "You've got two choices. Hold still and I'll give you a chance to explain, or it's out the door, and probably into Olson's bed. He'll blackmail you in a minute."

"He's got nothing on me, and he deserves everything he gets," she snapped back.

He reluctantly admired her style. She wasn't giving up easy. In a way, she reminded him of Fiona, his youngest sister, whom he'd pulled out of more scrapes than he could remember.

"But I do have something on you, Talia, a lot of somethings," he said quietly, logically, then left her to chew on that bone.

She opened her mouth, closing it as the sounds in the other room increased. After a time, Talia muttered, "That is disgusting."

Calum blew a strand of silky jasmine-scented hair away from his lips. Talia was in constant, if small, movement, her body brushing his with every turn. His lower body was heavy with need, much to his disgust. "Hold still," he ordered.

"Make me," she shot back.

Calum felt a small muscle contract in his cheek. "Fine," he said coolly before he lifted her jacket collar to a hook and hung her on the wall. He jerked a pillowcase from the shelf and tied her wrists; another pillowcase tied her ankles.

"Cute," she muttered darkly after a long moment.

"From your expression, I doubt that anyone has ever tried to make you do anything," he whispered over the faked sounds of the blonde's ecstasy. He rubbed his injured nose. Talia was a disaster, worse than a hurricane.

"You have no idea what I can do," she told him threateningly.

"That?" Calum asked, nodding toward the sounds.

His question was effective; her mouth clamped shut and she glared at him.

Calum leaned back against the wall. Temporarily safe from her kicks and elbows, he shot a quick inventory down his taut body and found it still aroused. The scent of jasmine enfolding him didn't help. He closed his eyes and wished for a nice, safe, logical problem. "I have no idea why I'm in this mess," he muttered to himself.

"There's no explaining nerd types," she answered in a logical tone, and then was quiet.

After a few more moments in which Calum tried to dismiss the amorous noises coming from the other room, he asked the question that had been grating on him. "Nerd?"

"Pocket protector. Glasses. Briefcase. Mind like a calculator. No fun at all. The good part is, you don't wear your belt up under your chest and your boring ties match."

"Thanks for that much." Calum closed his eyes. The air was filled with her womanly scent. He knew his nostrils were flaring, trying to catch every whiff. He hoped Olson would leave soon.

"Why are you so quiet?" she asked, long after the sounds of the room had stopped. "Can we leave?"

Calum wished he hadn't just remembered that the last time he was with a woman had been during his marriage. He'd grown used to accepting his quiet, well-ordered life—pre-Talia. "I want to get out of here just as bad as you do."

"Ah! That's because *now you're my accomplice*."

He glared at her. She was smirking. "Untie me, big boy. We're now birds of a feather that stick together."

"Hang there awhile and cool off. I think they're about to leave."

She blinked, clearly surprised. "That was quick. No after-sex cigarette in bed? They just get up and go? That isn't how it happens in the movies," she stated firmly, then flushed. "Well, that's not how *I* like it."

Calum stared at her for a second, then eased the door open, saw that the apartment was vacated and lifted Talia from her hook. Outside the closet, she waited patiently while he untied her. Then she leaped to the couch and placed her hands in a karate-style position. "Okay, let's have this out right now. You've messed up my caper. I'm not backing away from Olson until I have his big hairy nose quivering with fear. And I'm not letting you get away with hanging *me* on a hook, buddy."

Calum placed his hands on his hips and studied the woman bouncing as she waited for him to make his move. He shook his head and wished he hadn't been distracted by the soft flow of breasts beneath her black sweater. He studied her billowing mouse-colored hair and felt the muscle contract in his jaw. "I have to get away from you, or I will throttle you," he said as pleasantly as he could.

"Okay. Go. By the way, your hair is standing out in peaks and your glasses are crooked." She peered at him. "Hey, I think your jaw is swelling . . . maybe it's bruised. You should take better care of yourself. Maybe you're accident-prone. I'll see you in the morning and we can talk over old times, pal."

Calum ran his hands through his hair and straightened his glasses. "I should have—"

She shook her head. "It's my charm. Irresistible even to a nerd." Then she walked to the window, jammed it open and began to step out.

Calum grabbed the back of her jacket, and she turned on him. "I'm not going anywhere without my ropes and hooks."

He grabbed a fistful of the front of her jacket and pushed her back, controlling his strength because she was a woman. When he was on the ledge, he shook his head. Here he was, retrieving a blackmailer's scaling gear; he should have been dragging her to a police holding cell. Maybe he would, and then clean up the mess at Unique and—

Talia closed and locked the window, leaving him on the ledge. With a flourish, she jammed a small bit of plastic into the latch and wrapped the drapery cord around the lock handles so that they couldn't be picked. She drew out her camera, focused it on him and took his picture. She blew him a kiss and strolled out the door, her hair swaying down her back.

* * *

"This is my caper, and I'm not leaving because of a little push and shove from Iceman. Okay, okay... he was definitely heated last night, and definitely all man," Talia muttered to herself on her way to work the next morning, dressed in her usual disguise. She prepared the office and went to look for Calum Tallchief. Talia wanted to propose an offer that he couldn't resist—the problem was finding the right nerve. She doubted that Calum had soft spots—he *had* tied her up and hung her on a hook—but she pushed that thought aside, as well as the thought nudging her all night, that he wasn't aroused by her body.

She thought about disappearing—she could be very good at that. But she wanted Olson pinned to the wall.

When she didn't spot Calum, she swiftly left her office, carrying her big purse. The computer banks were on hold, humming nicely and waiting for work. Talia glanced out into the hallway and eased her purse open, her fingers finding the huge heavy-duty magnet.

Calum loomed beside her, looking just as cool as the day he had arrived. She noted a distinct glint behind his glasses, a rather smoldering, smoky look in his gray eyes. Talia's fingers released the magnet back into her purse. Calum plucked her purse from her, peered inside and shook his head. "Figures."

Then he walked off, placing the strap over his shoulder as if it were his bag.

Talia muttered her elephant-dung curse several times in his direction. She tried not to notice his long-legged stroll and his broad shoulders that narrowed down to lean hips. He reminded her of a mountain puma—big, graceful, solitary and powerful. And his male arrogance reminded her of the overprotective men in her family, the ones she had escaped at the first chance.

Talia deeply resented Calum's easy overpowering of her, and the way he had confined her. The closet episode had brought back her dislike of staying in one place for long and the boredom of tedious romantic commitments. At eighteen, she'd been a wide-eyed bride deserted at the altar; she'd been running ever since.

By 11:00 a.m., Olson had already stroked her arm and offered the first two sexual innuendos of the day. Alone at her desk, Talia traced the drawing of the ring Calum had given her. It was a lovely old thing, a Celtic design enclosing three large garnets. She checked off the name of her last query. If she could find that ring before he turned her in, she would have something he wanted. They could trade. He would go away, and she could continue—

Calum strolled into her cubicle, carrying a file folder and her purse. He tossed the purse, lightened by the removal of her best magnet, onto the desk and slapped the file down on it. "Read it and weep. You can buy me lunch, away from here. Set it up, or Olson will hear some interesting information about his secretary."

"You're enjoying this, aren't you, big boy?" She didn't trust his too-pleasant smile or his glinting eyes. She flipped open the file and ran her finger down the list of her misdemeanors, slight infractions that even Papa Petrovna didn't know about. Talia narrowed her eyes and growled quietly. If her own papa, the chief of police, didn't know she'd tampered with that politician's big television moment and rigged his slacks zipper to stay open, how could Calum?

Her family name, fingerprints, correct age—thirty-three—and life history spread before her. Her ship was sinking.

Darn. On top of that, Calum Tallchief had definitely sent sensual tingles up her spine. A closet spine-tingler. Trust a nerd to pull that one off.

Up close and disheveled, Calum had caused some unpredictable warmth and weakness in her legs. The sight of his gray eyes darkening as they locked on her bouncing breasts had stopped her.

She prayed for a bird of paradise to fly over and bomb Calum's black, arrogant head, then began furiously dialing pawnshops and antique shops. She got Nose—the street name of a man who was a human bloodhound—on the trail. At eleven-thirty, with no results, she closed her eyes and resigned herself to her fate. She made a luncheon reservation for Calum Tallchief and herself.

She chose a busy, jam-packed deli, and two sauce-dripping meatball sandwiches packed with onions. Dressed in an immaculate light blue suit, Calum looked perfectly at ease as he sat back, studying her. She noted with malice that he had managed his sandwich perfectly, while hers dripped steadily. She shifted uneasily within her hip padding and removed her knee from the intrusion of his hard one.

He tapped his fingers, and she jumped. "Is that a nerd method of Chinese water torture? *What?*"

"What." The word didn't have a question in it. It was flat and demanding.

"You know, Tallchief, I've always thought that nerds were flat-sided, one-dimensional. You turn them sideways and you've got nothing. No heart, no fun, nothing. What now?" she added tightly.

"Tell me why Talia Petrovna from Texas and other places has her mind on destroying Olson."

"The guy is a dog."

"True, but not good enough reason for your little disasters. Try again. You're just one step away from jail, Petrovna." His eyes skimmed past her fake mole, down to the rapid beat of her pulse. He reached out to strip off the mole, then dropped it to the floor. His expensive Italian loafer covered it.

She rubbed the slight burn on her neck; she didn't trust him. A guy who could spot fake moles wasn't normal. He moved too fast, and she didn't like his use of "little disasters." She had worked hard to bring down Olson; she had created beautiful, enormous disasters. "What's your motive? Do you think I'd tell you and give you the stuff to turn me in? No way."

"That's what I thought. That's exactly why you're taking a necessary leave of absence to visit your sick mother. Starting today. You're coming with me."

"Where?"

She didn't like his steely look, or any man giving her orders as if he had that right. "Look, guy. You may be enjoying this, but I'm not trading one slimeball for another. There's no way

you can blackmail me into sex. Jeez, I'm unqualified for nerd
sex. I think I feel faint—''

Calum slowly eased back the edge of his jacket. The pocket
protector and pens were missing. A small trickle of fear ran up
Talia's nape as he smiled blandly. He reminded her again of a
mountain cat—twitching its tail while waiting for her next
move. She sensed that he was enjoying their encounter. Talia
managed a threat. ''You don't have a chance with me, Tallchief. Remember—you were the one locked out on the ledge
last night. Not me.''

She allowed herself a smirk. ''I've got your picture, Mr.
Tallchief. Such a fierce, dark scowl. My, my...''

''Times change,'' he returned easily.

She deliberately peered at him. ''Do you know that you've
got the strangest movement in your jaw? The swollen side. Is
that a muscle contracting? A facial tic? Well, buddy, if you
think I won't make your life miserable, think again. Once I
finish Olson, I'm on to ruin your—''

''You're not making my day now,'' he interrupted her in a
low tone that caused her fingers to tremble on the pickle she
had stuck in her mouth. ''Are you going to eat that pickle
or—?'' He inhaled sharply. ''You're paying. Don't forget to
leave a tip.''

On the busy street, Talia dug her heels into the concrete.
Calum had a grip on her arm that didn't hurt, yet he managed to drag her along in his wake. Talia preferred to choose
her own path. ''I want my hooks and my ropes back. I paid a
fortune for them. Okay, I'll have to pay a fortune for them, if
I don't get them back to— Well, never mind. Someone who is
in the business. Rental fees are high on that stuff. I'm not going anywhere with you.''

She cursed in corrupted Russian as he walked off and she
was forced to run to keep up with him. He looked down at her
coolly before she could open her mouth. His glasses glinted
like round mirrors, and the sun caught blue sparks in his neatly
clipped hair as he said, very evenly, ''You're coming, you irritating little fireball, and one more curse from you, in whatever language, and I'll—''

Talia almost missed a step when his arm swung out and his hand rested lightly, possessively, on her waist. He easily drew her to his side. She had the miserable feeling that Calum would not give up easily, and that he'd chip away at her until he found her motive.

She emphasized the natural sway of her hips to test him. His reaction was immediate; his hand tightened on her padding, and his glance down at her was pure annoyance. She liked annoyance, but not the swift darkening of his eyes. Calum Tallchief, nerd, had definite warrior tendencies.

The sick-mother ploy worked easily. Especially when Talia's substitute from the secretarial pool appeared—tall, stacked and blond. The woman oozed a sexy welcome when she saw Calum Tallchief. "Disgusting," Talia muttered.

At nine o'clock that night, Calum looked in the rearview mirror at the car towed behind him. "Saboteurs shouldn't drive red convertible sports cars. Bad for a low profile."

Talia tugged at the handcuffs linking her to the four-wheeler. "So now you tell me. I never go anywhere without my car. I really didn't appreciate you plucking its poor little distributor cap off. I'm really good at that trick myself, so I knew where to look. Oh, and darlin', where did you put that, by the way?" she asked lightly. "In the back, with my things from the apartment? I've never had anyone move me before. So nice of you to save me the effort, and to be waiting for me to get off work. Now, about that distributor cap. If I were you, I really wouldn't mess with me on things like that. I don't like ramrods, or men who think they know what's best for me. I have a brain—I think."

In response he glanced at her disguise-dress and shook his head.

In the light of the dashboard, she noted that stubble darkened his jaw, giving him a dangerous look. The rolled-back sleeves exposed strong, hair-flecked forearms. A dark whorl of hair nestled in his opened shirt collar. The large hand easily moving the steering wheel looked as if it never released anything it wished to hold. She definitely sensed that she was being carried off to the dark, secret lair of a warrior. He seemed rather lonely at the office, prowling around like a Doberman, sniffing out her best-laid efforts. Her mother would probably want to bake him pies and fatten him. Jan would probably like him, and Alek and Anton would immediately take him into their hallowed male club, and Papa, too. When disturbed, Calum had...a dangerous edge, she decided. There was something magnificently male about him. *And she didn't like being controlled by overbearing males.*

She shivered and stared out into the night. She'd already had a sample of his strength and agility. Calum Tallchief moved fast, he was too smart, and he wasn't to be trusted. "You come close to me, Tallchief, and I'll break anything within reach."

He snorted; it was a disbelieving masculine sound.

"You know, a girl can't trust a guy who doesn't talk much. Communication can make friends." Talia leaned her head against the seat. She felt too drained to fight much tonight. Despite her dislike of Calum, there was a safety to him. He could easily have turned her in after the penthouse caper. Maybe she could work on some hidden gallantry, prey upon his sympathy, she thought sleepily. "I'd really like to know where we're going. A forwarding address for good old Mom, so she won't worry?"

"Go to sleep, Petrovna, and try not to curse me in whatever languages you've collected in your busy little life. After you tell me what I want to know, I'll know what to do next with you."

"Nice guy, Tallchief. Watch your toilet paper." Dozing, Talia thought she saw his mouth curve and smile lines crinkle beside his eyes.

Calum stretched in his cot, inhaling the fresh, cold morning air. He dozed, listening to the stream running not far from the cabin. October splashed the color of sunshine upon the Rockies' aspens and covered the tops of the mountains with snow. The deer were moving to lower meadows, and the warrior within him stirring.

This was his inheritance, his special place on Tallchief Mountain. In the shadowy single room, he opened his eyes to see Talia glaring at him. She looked nothing like the sleeping

woman he had carried inside the cabin. She had curled into
him as he lifted her from the seat and snuggled her face against
his throat. The delicious purring noises she made had reached
inside him, tormenting him.

He turned on his side and opened one eye to watch her tug
on the handcuff attached to her cot's post. A variety of clothing littered the floor, evidence that she had had difficulty in
finding the right escape outfit. Somehow she had managed to
shed the baggy dress and tug on very tight jeans that showed
every curve of her hips and long legs. She wore expensive running shoes, ready to leave immediately.

She moved, bending over, and Calum swallowed, his body
jerking to full alert.

Talia wore a bright blue top. The elastic strip across her
breasts revealed that she was not wearing a bra and that every
curve was all woman. Calum swallowed again. Above the
elastic, her breasts flowed with each tug. Calum's body responded almost painfully. He closed his eyes; she was a disaster.

He groaned mentally and tried not to notice the delicate
jasmine scent that had filled his cabin during the night. The
subtle scent had aroused him, wafting gently through the
smells of wood smoke.

She glanced his way and continued to drag the cot stealthily
after her, making her way toward his slacks, slung over a
wooden chair. "Going somewhere?" Calum asked lightly.

She straightened immediately, her eyes rounded innocently.
Her handcuffed hand clutched the cot's post. "Who, me?"

Dressed in jeans and nothing else, he stood up quickly,
stretched and put on his glasses. The careless stretch and yawn
had taken great effort; his body ached, rigid in every muscle,
with sexual need. He didn't appreciate his body's awakening
to Talia's.

Talia stared at him. She looked down his body, then up
again. "Nerds don't wear jeans," she said, as if stating a well-
known fact. "Not worn ones with light spots in appropriate
male areas. Or ones that hang low with the front snap open.

My auntie Em, Calum! You're tan all over, and you've got...*muscles!*''

She took a deep breath as he moved to uncuff her and to easily shove the cot back against the wall. ''You're not fitting the perfect nerd picture, Tallchief.''

He tried to ignore her dipping elastic top and the crevice of her breasts. Her rounded eyes on his body had every nerve dancing on sensual alert. Then, shaking his head, he reached to quickly tug up her top. The brush of her silky breast remained on his fingers after they slid away. He shook his head again as Talia backed up against the wooden door, her hands behind her. She smiled sweetly at him and batted her lashes. ''No phone, darlin'. How do I dial room service?''

Calum knew he'd feel better after coffee, and he began to quickly stoke the old stove. ''The door has a hidden lock, Talia. Save your energy. And...put...on...a shirt.'' He tossed one of his to her.

The next instant, Calum ran his hands over his face. The image of Talia in his shirt wasn't helping his temporarily unstable need to fit her body against his. He glanced at the smooth sway of her hips and knew she walked like no other woman he'd known. She had a walk that would easily draw men's eyes, and Calum didn't intend to be one of her conquests. Talia's sexuality was like her perfume—invasive, feminine and unwanted. He concentrated on preparing their meal. He didn't intend to come close to that illogical, sexual flash point with a volatile woman like Talia. Ever.

Calum frowned. He would choose his encounters logically, and Talia wasn't on that schedule.

Talia wandered around the cabin, peering out the windows, while he prepared biscuits, eggs and bacon. She ate ravenously, and daintily reached to take his last strip of bacon. She munched on it and eyed him with speculation. ''Okay. I'm ready to confess. The way I figure it, you'll be considered as my accomplice now. How did you explain your absence from the job?''

''Logically. I needed a few days to research leads.'' Calum noted the cream and sugar she poured into her coffee. ''Are you going to drink that or play with it?''

"I like sweet things, Tallchief. And nice guys. Listen, I might as well tell you up front, don't torture me. I've never thought I'd be good at that. If you've brought me here, to God knows where, to let the chipmunks listen to my screams, I'd rather not frighten the wildlife. If you don't mind."

Calum crushed the paper napkin in his hand. He'd brought her here to protect her from herself. Now the idea seemed insane. "Petrovna, the thought appeals."

Talia leaned forward, and Calum tried to force his eyes away from the deep crevice between her breasts. She seemed unaware of how she could stir male needs. Calum decided that was a practiced skill, just as Sherry's had been. No woman would be that unaware of how badly a man could want her, how the small cabin intensified needs—

Talia looked at him intently. "You're up the creek, Tallchief. You've done the deed. We're in cahoots now." Then she spoke slowly, distinctly, as if explaining to a child. "You're in this with me. Together we could really do a number on old Sleazeball. We could avenge every woman he's taken advantage of."

Calum couldn't remember when any woman had distracted him the way Talia did. The thought was disconcerting. The rumpled bed behind her set him on edge. He could easily see tossing her upon it.

Calum scowled at her graceful fingers. He realized how his great-great-grandfather Tallchief must have felt when he tried to toss Una onto the tepee pelts. Calum had never tossed a woman beneath him, nor would he. He pushed the illogical thought aside and met Talia's narrowed eyes.

"Why did you bring me here, Tallchief?" she asked warily.

"You might not believe this, but you remind me of my sister." She had reminded him of Fiona, when he first discovered what she was trying to do. But in the same cabin with her, and after a discussion with her brother, Alek Petrovna, that motive shredded to bits. "Fiona is always trying to protect someone, something. But you were in a position to get hurt badly, or prosecuted. I wanted to give you a chance."

"Oh, right. Uh-huh. Sure. Mr. Galahad to the rescue. I don't trust you. You're on Olson's payroll."

"So are you." Calum found his fingers locked around Talia's wrist. The woman raised his hackles, and he resented it. "Now you. You've gone to a tremendous amount of work. Why?"

She tried to tug her hand away. "Oh, nothing to do. Bored, I guess."

He released her wrist slowly. "Olson has really stepped on your bad side, hasn't he? Did you know one of the women?"

She sat back and crossed her arms over her chest. "You can't make me talk. *Unless* you agree that you're with me. That you'll either help me, or ignore what you find. I've got people to protect in this caper."

Her expression softened as she ran her finger around the rim of her coffee mug. Calum realized that whoever had her thoughts at that moment also had a portion of her heart. The tiny well of jealousy springing up in him shocked him. He hadn't found a lover in his background check on Talia Petrovna, though he'd learned that men drooled after her. It didn't help his nerves to know that he was one of those men. "I'll do my job, and you, Miss Talia Petrovna, will eventually tell me what I want to know. By the way, did you return those hooks and ropes to Vinnie the human fly?"

She smiled coolly and met his eyes. "Fingerprints again, I suppose. You rat, you found Vinnie by lifting his prints. Now that is low-down and devious."

"You'll do the dishes if you want any more food, Petrovna." Much as he resented that his protective instincts seemed locked on this woman and that she little appreciated what it could cost him, Calum found a primitive excitement racing through him that he didn't trust. He realized that at some level, Talia affected his warrior instincts; his logic told him that the whole matter was nonsense.

His body told him differently.

She leveled a meaningful stare at him. "If you know what's good for you, you'll give me my distributor cap and send me on my way. If you don't let me go, you have absolutely no idea what I am capable of."

Calum studied her set face. He knew what she would do once he released her. He wasn't ready to let her go. Something deep inside him wanted to prolong his Talia Petrovna misery. "You'll go straight back to mayhem, sabotage and Olson."

"You've got it, Sherlock." She lifted an eyebrow. "There's no way you could have gotten that information on me unless you contacted someone I know very well. Say a family member. Someone I grew up with."

He sipped his coffee and waited. Without the tinted contact lenses, Talia's blue eyes darkened as she glared at him. He watched with interest, as she seemed to be building up to explode, which she did. She threw a cup against the wall. It rattled across the floor as she glared at Calum. "Alek Petrovna is a rat! Don't believe anything my brother says! How much did he tell you?" she asked warily.

"What was in the file, and he asked me to keep you safe. He said you'd tell me the rest. I'm waiting." Alek hadn't asked, he had yelled and demanded that his little sister be in one happy piece the next time he saw her. He expected regular reports, and he had put Calum through an investigation that was tight and thorough, with double checks. Alek was extremely protective of Talia, and he'd promised torture if anything happened to his little sister.

The passion coloring Talia's cheeks and lighting her eyes fascinated Calum. She was a symphony of color and movement.

Talia shook her head and closed her eyes. "Okay. I'll take care of Alek, right after I take care of you, right after I take care of Olson."

"That's a long list."

"I'm up to it."

Three

___

Calum tried to keep his attention on his computer screen. He systematically ran through Tallchief investments and tried to keep his mind off the pacing, furious woman sharing his cabin. With difficulty, he forced his eyes from the elegant sway of Talia's hips to thoughts of her sister, Jan—January Petrovna. Alek had not offered information about his youngest sister; Calum was certain that Talia's revenge had something to do with Jan, who he'd discovered had worked for Olson.

At odds with her striking looks, Talia's financial savvy fascinated Calum. Her wise investments provided her with an uncommon income and allowed her the freedom of mobility—to step into trouble at will. Talia invested cautiously and took risks. Her game style was unique and profitable; she wasn't the simple headstrong go-for-it woman as she appeared.

Alek Petrovna had not been difficult to locate. A call to his wire service about his busy sister, and Alek had called immediately from a war-torn country. Concerned about his sister, the tough journalist had yelled over a bombardment of shells.

He'd checked out Calum's credentials within minutes and wired the information needed about Talia. He'd promised to check up on his little sister and roared with laughter when Calum described her antics.

Yet Alek had not revealed Talia's motives, and he hadn't said much about Jan.

The fire crackled in the stove, warding off the cold weather. By midafternoon, Talia had stopped threatening Calum, though he had begun to appreciate her creativity. She was too quiet, sitting on her cot and watching the afternoon mixture of rain and early snow trickle down the window. From the shadows, she'd been studying him closely, seeking out his weak points. Now she was somewhere else, and the expression on her face was soft, with a whimsical curve to her lips. Her slender, pale fingers traced the rain trails slowly; she was the image of a vanquished challenger. He wondered what her next move would be.

Her last one had been to hurl another cup at him. He'd caught it and smiled tightly. "Thanks. I was just getting ready for some more."

He clicked off the computer and stared at her.

After a moment, she stared back, her expression hardening. The light touched the angles of her face, softening her fierce expression.

"Okay. You want to do this the hard way, Petrovna?" Calum began. "We'll do it the hard way." He began to mentally arrange his questions about her motives.

Ignoring him, she stood up, jerked off his shirt and began to stretch. She parted her legs and eased her body to one side, touching the toes of one foot, then the other. The warm-up exercises caused Calum to inhale, every molecule in his body locked on the flow and rhythm of Talia's. So much for his plans. He wanted her; his body was taut. "I'm going outside."

She continued to ignore him, and Calum stepped outside. He realized that he had slammed the door; he realized that he was standing in the freezing rain, shivering, when the cabin belonged to him. He stepped back inside to find Talia rummaging through his traveling bag. He leaned against the door and folded his arms over his chest. At least the movement kept his hands from reaching for her delectable neck. "The distributor cap isn't there."

"Cut the chitchat, Tallchief. I'm not in the mood." She began to run in place.

Calum forced his gaze to remain above her shoulders, on the irritating angle of her stubborn chin. "You're a spoiled little witch who has run amok your entire life. You've got your father and brothers and every other male you've come in contact with under your thumb." He paused for effect. "But you are not going back to destroy yourself."

"Alek will pay," she returned grimly. "It must have been easy to connect him with me, given a name like Petrovna."

Then Talia paused, looked at Calum thoughtfully and grabbed a towel, blotting it across her forehead.

Calum watched her glide toward him, taking away his breath. Talia placed one hand on the door, beside his head, and smoothed his hair with the tip of her finger.

Calum found himself holding his breath and relishing her next move. The woman intrigued and fascinated him, despite his aversion to problem people. Talia had Problem pasted all over her. He fought falling into the warm scents of jasmine and overheated woman enticing him.

She studied his face and ran the tip of her finger over his ear. She touched his bottom lip and trailed her finger down his chin. "You know, this could be fun. Together, we could level Olson."

"Fun?" Though Calum kept his expression steady, every nerve in him wanted to paste Talia's body against his. He wanted to feed upon that generous soft mouth—

"Mmm . . . Think about it." Then she turned slowly and walked away from him, the sway of her long, straight hair almost brushing her hips.

Calum closed his eyes, shook his head and forced himself to concentrate on how he was getting out of this mess. He'd always been in charge of his life, but for one dizzying moment, he'd felt like a butterfly on the tip of a pin, or a moth drawn toward a light.

Calum shook his head. At two hundred pounds and more, he was no butterfly-moth. And there was no reason he was here with this maddening woman. He hadn't thought out a plan; he'd simply captured her and whisked her to safety. Olson wasn't getting her.

He grimly decided to blame his actions on the Tallchief males' protective genes.

"There are big wild animals out there," Talia stated slowly, watching the night through the window. "What are they?"

"Take your pick...moose and bear. A hungry wolf or two." Calum resented how Talia looked now, her face pale, her eyes shadowed and rounded. She seemed deceptively fragile. Her slight torment should have pleased him; it didn't. With her hair in a ponytail and dressed in his shirt and her jeans, she looked like a young girl. He could deal with the girl image and keep Talia on a level with Fiona.

Like hell.

Talia had skin like silk, she walked like no other woman, and every molecule of him heated just from looking at her.

She moved closer to him. "I want to go home, Tallchief."

Calum turned off his computer and looked at her steadily. "We can go anytime you tell me what I want to know. And when I have your word that you will leave Olson alone."

She glared back. "You'll pay," she said finally. "Petrovna's Law. I am very good at what I do."

He lifted an eyebrow. "You think it's pleasant being in your vicinity? Tell me what I want to know and we'll work from there."

A coyote howled and, with a fearful gasp, Talia hurled herself against him. She wrapped her arms around him and shivered, just once. Calum found his arms locking around her, resisting slightly as she stepped back. She stared at him. "Sorry. I forgot you're the enemy."

Calum dealt with the immediate need to lay her down and love her. She glanced at him resentfully. "Okay, okay. Stop glaring at me. You're big and hard and strong, and I got scared for just a second. It won't happen again. Just how long do you plan to keep me here? You should know that nothing is going to keep me from ruining Olson. Nothing.''

"I am," Calum stated quietly. He forced himself not to look at the slope of her breast where her shirt had come unbuttoned.

"Darlin', the day some paid-for hit man stops me, that's the day I'll turn it in for an apron and a houseful of kiddies.''

"Don't press your luck." Calum almost smiled at the image. *Exotic* described Talia, like a colorful butterfly. He couldn't see her in the role of a housewife.

When Calum stepped outside for firewood, he returned to the door to find it wouldn't budge. He pushed his shoulder against the wood and pushed slowly, forcing it open. Behind it, objects crashed, furniture slid and Talia cursed. Within minutes, Talia had stacked the contents of the cabin against the door. He stepped over a chair, then over a cot mattress, and neatly placed the firewood in the box. In a blur of motion, Talia raced by him, out into the freezing rain.

Her athletic stride took her quickly down the rough road. Calum was faster, and when he reached her, they went down into the mud and the snow. A thrill like none he'd ever known before shot through him; he'd captured a woman he wanted very much. He stopped breathing, focused on her and exhaled sharply. He shook his head to clear it; he preferred a sensible life—without Talia.

"Get off me, you big lug," she stated between heaving breaths that dragged her breasts up to his chest. She squirmed beneath him. Calum discovered he'd firmly inserted his leg between hers. The movement startled him; it was primitive and possessive. His body flexed in reaction, his thigh pressing higher as she glared at him. "Now you've gotten me dirty."

"I ought to—" Beneath the layers of sweatshirts and the heavy coat, he felt her body against his. A tropical heat surged through Calum, stunning him.

Calum held very still, too aware that his thumbs were stroking the fine inner skin of her wrists. He realized that he was lying between her legs and that her thighs were quivering along his.

In the next second, he was on his feet, his chest heaving as he tried to calm the need to crush her mouth beneath his. He locked his knees to stop the shaking of his body, wrapped his fist in the jacket she had taken and pulled her slowly to her feet. He lowered his face to hers and spoke very softly. "Get back to the house."

Talia stared at him for a moment. She fluttered her lashes, taunting him. "But, master, I'm dirty, and there's no bathroom there."

"We'll manage," he returned tightly before giving her a light shove toward the cabin.

While Talia was bathing in a tub of heated water behind a wall of blankets, Calum shook his head. He found himself close to muttering, something he'd never done before meeting Talia. The cabin was warm, steaming, and scented of female flesh. Calum ran his hands over his face and grimaced when he felt the bruise she had left on him from the window incident.

When she placed her bare feet on the floor, Calum found his gaze locked on her ankles, revealed by the blanket. His hands could wrap around them easily. She was humming, and the blanket moved as she bumped it. Talia emerged, dressed in hot-pink pants and a tight long-sleeved pink sweater. Calum's mouth went dry at the sight of her nipples, thrusting at the knit fabric. A sensual punch landed in his midsection and slid lower, lodging heavily and uncomfortably in an area he considered very private. She closed her eyes, giving herself to the erotic motion of drying her hair with a towel. "Oh, this is good. The first time I get into a real bathroom, I'm having a soak that will last two days."

The purring, sensuous noises she made as she dried her hair weren't helping the rising desire within him.

He wondered whether she purred when she made love, and his body lurched into desire.

She was very quiet as he handcuffed her to the cot. He didn't trust her innocent, friendly smile, and he took his bath quickly, sliding into clean jeans and drawing on a thermal shirt. He shot her a warning glance as he turned off the light.

After a night of his body hardening each time her cot creaked, Calum finally fell into a fitful sleep. When he awoke, the room was freezing. A bottle, nudged by the wind, rolled across the table and hit the floor. Talia's cot was empty, and the window was not tightly closed.

He found her expertly hot-wiring his four-wheeler.

The next evening, Talia sat on her side of his vehicle. Calum Tallchief was interesting, once she'd peeled back his sleek edges. She noted that occasionally now he muttered a bit. In her experience with Petrovna males, muttering was good—a sign that she was getting to them, wearing down their overbearing, controlling behavior.

This guy was big and bleak and tasty. Not that she'd ever really tasted a man, except for a few really indulgent and unsatisfying kisses. Deep within Talia Petrovna lurked an old-fashioned girl, raised with traditional family rules. Only her family knew that despite her travels and antics, she was basically old-fashioned. An outdated good girl. Alek and Anton loved to point that out to her. They tactfully avoided references to her one try at a wedding—the one at which she'd been jilted at the altar.

But Calum raised a certain challenge, and she never passed up a really good one. What woman could ignore Calum's towering wall of dark, tangy secrets? She was certain that pain lurked in his past, and— Darn, that brought out the need to comfort him again.... As if human Dobermans could be cuddled. Still, when first seen in the mornings, with his hair rumpled, his body aroused against his tight jeans, and his magnificent chest ... If she wasn't anxious to destroy Olson, she might—

Talia glanced at Calum's profile. Right now, he was singed around the edges—a minor mishap during her first experience with a wood stove. The pink sunset traced his angular, hard face as he turned to lift one black-singed eyebrow at her. She smiled tentatively. "Now tell me your master scheme again, darlin'."

He slashed a steely look at her, then back at the winding road. "We're going to Tallchief Mountain in Amen Flats. It's a wide spot in the road, and every one knows me. I'll tell everyone you're my new housekeeper. Basically, I'm keeping you away from Olson, until we come to a working solution—''

"You want to wear me down. Better men than you have tried, Tallchief. To you a working solution is that old, dull theme about me letting Olson get away with—''

"What?"

She inhaled and looked into the fading light. At every turn, Calum was there, pushing, needling her. "Handcuffs won't cut it. I'm gone the minute I can. Meanwhile, you can tell me about your love life."

She loved Calum's glower. He was responding nicely to her careful pricks. He didn't like her prowling through his private life. She'd have him turning her loose any minute. "You've been married, right?"

"Hmm . . . Why don't we talk about Jan now?"

His level, too-quiet tone startled her. She should have known. Calum had been very busy, digging into her family secrets. "Jan?" she asked innocently, hoping that Calum wouldn't know too many details.

"January Petrovna, your baby sister. Now married and separated from Roy Johnson. She went back to Texas, and he's still in Denver. Recently she worked for Olson for a few months before they separated. Roy won't talk, but he's a mess and still in love."

"When did you talk to him?"

"Just after I ran an identification check on Jan. It was the day I ran your fingerprints."

"My compliments. You're just full of surprises." Talia swallowed and stared at Calum's profile. The line of his jaw was unrelenting, even as he flicked a glance at her. *Way too dangerous,* she decided. Calum Tallchief was no nerd.

When she tested him at the cabin, pinning him against the wall, she'd wanted to take the smooth rock nestled on his chest and draw him to her. Calum's eyes had gone the color of night smoke then, and she'd known that she was fighting him on a basic level she did not understand.

Talia shifted uneasily in her seat. "Okay. Okay, I'll be your housekeeper. Temporarily. I know . . . your bird dog reputation will suffer if anything happens to Olson while you're on the job. I can understand why you'd want to clear yourself, darlin'."

She thought she saw Calum's grim mouth curl in satisfaction. "Stop calling me *darlin'*," he ordered quietly.

"Tell me about Amen Flats and Tallchief Mountain," she shot back.

"The town is small and the mountain is big," he stated, easily handling his four-wheeler around a sharp curve.

"Let's cut to the base rules—no sex."

His look down her body was slow, and it raised the heat in Talia's body. "Now why would you think I'd be interested? Count me out, lady. You're not my type."

She flushed. *Now that was a definite challenge.* She wondered what was his type. Whoever it was had left him aching. Though he was big and brooding and edgy after getting singed, Talia had the strange impulse to hold him and comfort him. She watched a city limits sign slide past—Amen Flats, population 4,000. "You're not my idea of fun, either, Tallchief."

"You know, Petrovna, you always have the last word. Someday you won't." Calum pulled his four-wheeler down Amen Flats's main street, which was really a state highway. Everyone in Maddy's Hot Spot had their noses pasted to the window, wondering about the little sports car behind his. From their expressions, it looked as if Birk and Lacey were already moving into an argument about the car and how fast it could race. He noted their motorcycles parked in front of the tavern. He wasn't the only one; Talia's stare had locked on to the fast, elegant beasts. "Don't even think about it. I know you placed first in the High Mud Bike Ride."

She smiled innocently at him and fluttered her lashes. "I have other skills. You'll be sorry if you provoke me into using them."

He reeked of the smoke that Talia's diversion had caused in the cabin. Before the stove had burst into a small flame. A particle of soot fluttered from his head to his nose, and Calum blew it away. Another night with Talia and he'd be— Calum rubbed his hand over his unshaven jaw. His hand came away coated with soot.

His home, a sleek, modern wooden affair with a rambling yard, settled into the evening shadows of Amen Flats. It didn't surprise him that the lights were on in the house and Elspeth was waiting for him at the gate. She carried a woven lunch basket. Elspeth always sensed his homecomings; he could almost taste fresh bread and a tasty casserole. He shot a glance at Talia, who was studying Elspeth. "She's my sister. Be nice," he ordered curtly as he stopped the vehicle.

"Aren't I always?" Talia asked sweetly before opening her door and sliding out. She moved toward Elspeth gracefully, purposefully, and the hair on Calum's nape lifted. He hurried to her side. "Elspeth, this is Talia Petrovna. She's going to keep house for me. For a time."

Talia smiled warmly, and Calum blinked. Her smile could have charmed Duncan's mean longhorn bull into acting like a frisky calf. "I'm so pleased to meet you, Elspeth."

She looked away from Elspeth's quiet stare, which moved slowly to Calum, then back to Talia. "Aye." Elspeth's voice was as soft as her gaze upon her brother, who shifted restlessly. "Aye," she said again, in a tone of approval.

"Nay," Calum shot back darkly. "Not in a trillion years."

"Petrovna, did you say?" Elspeth frowned slightly, as though tracking the name through her memory.

"Yes. My brother is Alek Petrovna, a journalist. You may have heard of him."

Elspeth hesitated, then answered lightly, "Perhaps." Elspeth looked as though she knew something that Calum or Talia did not. "I'm pleased that you've come here," Elspeth said quietly.

"For a time," Talia stated.

"A short time," Calum added firmly.

Talia's smile was angelic. She flicked a particle of soot from his ear and reached up to pat his head. "Calum is helping me between jobs."

"Mmm... I see," Elspeth murmured, rising on tiptoe to hug and kiss her brother. She stood back, smothering a grin. "Calum, you smell like smoke, but your singed look is becoming. I don't believe I've ever seen you so...distracted." She studied him. "Strange."

"Calum got all bothered when I turned the damper on the stove. There was a bit of smoke, and a teeny fire. He has a murderous temper, you know. I couldn't help it that his clothes got a little scorched. He shouldn't have tried to put out the fire by himself," Talia informed her, and smiled sweetly at Calum. "He mutters, you know. Who would have thought it?"

"I do *not* mutter." The fire had been her last ploy at the cabin, the turning point at which he decided that he couldn't stand another night with her tossing in her cot.

Or watching the very feminine sway of her hips. Now that they'd moved to his house, he hoped she would do her mind-stopping exercises in the privacy of her room.

While the small holes of his clothes were still smoldering, Calum had almost picked her up and—for just that instant, he almost tossed her on the cot.... Talia had glared at him, curiously unaware of the sensual danger he presented. Curiously. Almost naive about his painful need of her, especially when her hand had brushed his thigh and pressed against him as she squirmed.

That hand had stopped him. On the cusp of pressing it firmly against his body, Calum had managed to push her away.

"Strange," Elspeth murmured with an impish smile. "We call him Calum the cool."

Talia laughed outright. "Calum the cool. I'll remember that. By the way, tell me about Duncan."

"Duncan the defender." Elspeth's tone was affectionate. "He's our older brother, and until now I thought *he* was the dark, moody one."

"Calum is just having a bad hair day. Tell me more about your family, Elspeth."

"No." Calum released the breath he had been holding and pushed his hand through his singed hair. "Not tonight."

Talia fluttered her lashes. "Petrovna's Law includes tit for tat. Elspeth, what is this about a family ring? I'm helping Calum find it. I understand you traced it to Denver."

Calum stared at the mountains and rocked on his heels. Somewhere there was a world without Talia, a quiet, steady, predictable world.

"Our great-great-grandmother had to sell her dowry to keep Tallchief Mountain. We've each pledged to bring back one item. Calum's search is for the ring." Elspeth smiled at Calum meaningfully. "The Tallchief dowry has legends."

When a man of Fearghus blood places the ring upon the right woman's finger, he'll capture his true love forever.

Elspeth didn't have to voice the legend; it hovered in the crisp October air between them. Calum didn't like the amused light in her eyes as she turned to Talia. "You must be tired. There's supper waiting in the warming oven, and I hope you like your room. I put some bath salts near the tub and laid out fresh towels. I need to get back to my weaving now. I have a new order of shawls waiting to be filled. I'll check to see if you need anything tomorrow. Good night, Talia. Calum." Then she moved gracefully into the shadows.

"She's beautiful," Talia murmured. "There's something very different about her...soothing. I like her. How did you manage to call her and tell her I'd be coming?" She eyed him darkly. "Don't tell me you had this whole thing planned."

"I didn't call her. Elspeth just knows." He didn't like explaining his family to Talia.

"Really? She's a psychic? What do you know about that! And in such a tiny town, too. What do people do here for excitement?"

Calum watched as Talia studied the rugged, snowcapped mountains in the distance, turning as she looked out over Amen Flats. Then she turned to his house, studying the angular contemporary shape, his own design. "Where's the big, tough black yard dog? A perfect pet for you."

"I don't have pets."

"Mmm...Women?"

"Stop pushing." She nettled him. He could have any number of pets if he wanted them. Female clutter didn't fit his life-style. Calum followed her up the walkway with a sinking feeling. He tried not to notice the distinctive feminine sway of her hips. In a half hour, everyone in Amen Flats would know that he had brought a woman home. Even now, the telephone lines were probably hot with the news.

For now, he had Talia on a tether. And he had no idea why he had placed his professional reputation in danger. He found himself staring at Talia's hips as she ascended the stairs, heading straight for the bathroom. He closed his eyes and shook his head. He needed sleep; his nerves were drawn too tight. The sooner he was rid of Talia Petrovna, the sooner he could get his life back on track. He waited until he heard the bathwater running, and then he began to make calls.

Talia emerged from the bath; she now felt up to battling Calum. "You've got quite the little security system here. Not that I tried the windows or anything... It's a wonder what a bath can do for a girl—"

Calum, freshly showered, stood waiting for her at the bottom of the steps. He took her breath away. Water gleamed on his coal-black hair—a drop caught on his bare chest—and the smooth black stone gleamed on the leather thong. There was a primitive edge to Calum Tallchief, one she wanted to explore. In jeans, with his shirt opened, Calum was all sexy male.

Until she looked at his scowl, his black eyebrows jammed together and the muscle contracting in his jaw. His eyes dropped to midway on her chest, and he shook his head. She glanced down at the nightshirt she loved; it was worn thin and revealed her breasts. She instantly crossed her arms. She'd never been shy about skimpy clothing, but then, she'd never met a man like Calum. He caused her to feel very feminine and aware of how much she'd like his mouth on hers. She remembered his weight between her legs as they lay in the mud and the snow. The movement of his thigh nudging her intimately was firm and knowledgeable. She'd danced away from men who pursued her too closely; Calum had the look of a hunter, of a man not easily put off.

Talia inhaled sharply. She didn't like being pushed and locked into corners. Out of his business suit and clearly at home, Calum wore his warrior arrogance like a big danger flag.

"Here. Put this on. You look cold." He took off his shirt and tossed it to her. He watched grimly as she put it on. "Button it."

He lifted a pale strand of her hair, studying it in the fire-light. She sensed that he could easily wrap his hand in it and tug her to him. Talia eased back slightly as he studied the various light shades. "A blonde. I should have known you'd dyed your hair."

"I've always liked basic brown. Goes with everything. But it was time for a change." Talia inhaled the scents of soap and freshly showered male. The cloth was still warm from his body. When she made no move to button it, but met his gaze, Calum moved closer and began to button the shirt. She studied his big hands, moving slowly, efficiently down the cloth, and wanted his touch upon her. She moved closer, watching him now as his knuckles brushed her softness. She reacted instantly, her nipples peaking, shocking her. When his eyes darkened to the shade of night smoke and flickered down to her breasts, her heart stilled.

Talia found her hand opened on his chest, her fingers pale against the black hair and darkly tanned skin. Beneath her palm, Calum's heart pounded in a fascinating rhythm, drawing her to him. Talia moved instinctively, as she always did. She caught the black stone around his neck in her fist, pressed her body against his and rested her head upon his chest. He felt good—warm, steady, comfortable. She nuzzled the hard padding of his chest and inhaled more of his delicious scents.

A telephone rang somewhere, and Talia was left standing and swaying without Calum's support. She frowned at him as he answered the telephone. No man had ever moved away from her. *That's my role,* she decided, slightly outraged. Of course, she'd never reacted to a man as she had to Calum. She glared at him. He didn't know anything about her rules, but he would learn.

Calum scowled back at her from the kitchen, looking dark and dangerous as he pressed the receiver to his ear. "Fiona, why are you calling?" His eyes flickered to Talia as she moved closer and waited, hoping to hear more. He turned away, presenting her with an expanse of broad back that fascinated her. She reached out a finger to stroke a muscle running across his shoulder blade, and he looked down at her over his shoulder. "Yes, I brought a woman home. We're here together. She's going to keep house for me. No, I didn't find the ring yet, but I will. Yes. I just told you that I brought her home. Hell, no, I'm not like Duncan carrying off the woman I want—" He glanced impatiently at Talia, who was standing very close. "Would you mind?"

"No," she returned innocently, and eased closer. "Just how many women have you carried off to your cave?" The jolt of jealousy surprised her. She dismissed it as anger at the man temporarily foiling her plans.

Calum inhaled and spoke into the telephone, "Fiona, we'll talk later, okay? And stay out of trouble. Montana is a big state. Find a cause to keep you busy. Call me when it's bail-bond time."

Talia watched, fascinated, as Calum's expression softened. "I worry about you, too. Don't forget to call when you need me."

"Girlfriend?" Talia asked as she followed him into the kitchen.

"Sister." Calum began cutting warm bread, and Talia couldn't wait to butter it.

"Is this real homemade butter?" she asked, munching away while Calum placed a hot casserole on the table.

"You could help."

"Help what?" she asked between delicious bites of buttery warm bread.

"Set the table. You're supposed to be my housekeeper."

Calum stared at her mouth, and Talia found her heartbeat kicking up to warp speed. "So you said. I think it's sweet how you thought of my reputation. How many women have you had here?" she heard herself ask. If other women had seen Calum's dark smoky look in this same house...if he had buttoned them into his shirt...such a sweet, protective gesture...she'd— His gaze had fallen to her mouth and lingered, warming it. She licked a crumb from her bottom lip as he traced the movement.

Unprotected from the sudden lurch of her heart, Talia glanced at the assortment of small potted plants on the cabinet. Munching on her bread and butter, she moved toward them and away from Calum. The tiny, fragrant leaves bobbed beneath her light touch.

"Herb starts from Elspeth. She likes to give things she likes—" Calum glanced out into the night, and then at Talia, as if wondering where he could stash her. When a light knock at the door sounded, his deep voice was almost a snarl, and he moved in front of Talia, almost protectively, backing her into a corner of the cabinet. She hopped up and sat on the counter, one hand on his tense shoulder and the other holding her buttered bread. She liked touching him.

A man as tall as Calum, but more heavily built, entered the kitchen. He wore his grim look like a cloak, though his eyes— the shade of Calum's—lit with amusement.

"Hi. I'm Talia. Mmm... Interesting," she managed around a mouthful of delicious bread. "He looks just like you, Calum. Same steel-colored eyes, same dark skin and black hair, same— I like the cowboy getup. Boots, hat, gloves... Mmm... Is that apple pie?"

"Fresh from the oven. My wife, Sybil, sent it for you. She'll be over in the morning with Megan, our daughter. Emily, our other daughter, will stop by on her way from school, if that's okay."

"I'd love to meet everyone. Calum has told me so much about the Tallchief family," she lied.

"So you've finally caught one, Calum. Elspeth said it would be soon." The other man's voice held amusement. He removed his hat in a lovely cowboy gesture and nodded to Talia. "Ma'am, I apologize for my little brother. He's not usually so poor-mannered. I'm his big brother, Duncan."

Talia leaned to whisper in Calum's ear. "I like him. He's sweet."

Calum moved back slightly, and his large hands found her knees, resting beside his hips. She concentrated on the erotic circles his thumbs were drawing on the inside of her knees.

Talia reached across Calum's shoulder, extending her hand for Duncan's handshake. "Calum has had a bad day. He's tired," she explained sweetly, and noted that Calum had tensed immediately.

Duncan chuckled. "Elspeth said he was slightly singed when you arrived. He had soot in his hair."

Talia noted the muscle leaping in Calum's jaw as he said, "Put the pie on the table. Thank Sybil for me, and—"

Calum stood very still as Talia draped her arms around his shoulders. "I'm his very own live-in housekeeper," she said teasingly, while blowing in his ear.

Duncan burst out in guffaws. Calum's skin heated beneath her touch in a slight but noticeable blush. "I want pie," Talia stated over the wild thumping of her heart. But with Calum's muscled back nestled against her, she wondered whether she didn't want another dessert—one with a protective, rather sweet attitude.

Four

When the sun rose the next morning, Talia began shoving away the furniture she had placed against her bedroom door. She accidentally dropped a chair and bit her lip, pressing her ear to the door. With luck, Calum would be sleeping, or engrossed in his computer, and she could make it to his vehicle—

"Can I help?" The masculine drawl stopped Talia. She sat heavily upon the old chest and shook her head. The door opened; she gripped the chest as it began to slide across the floor, carrying her. She hopped off as Calum leaned against the door and nudged her carryall bag aside with her toe. His eyes ran down her black sweater and leggings. She'd added the Hessian boots as a touch of her passionate and daring Russian inheritance. Calum wasn't the only one with dynamic ancestors. She always felt up to any caper dressed in black and with her hair neatly tucked in a single waist-length braid.

"Oh! Hello. Just a little furniture arranging. I hope you don't mind. I put rugs beneath the legs so as not to scar the beautiful wood flooring." She eyed Calum's bare chest and the corded arms crossed upon it. The black obsidian, secured by the leather thong, nestled on gleaming coarse hair. Her fingertips tingled with the need to grab that stone and tug his mouth to hers.

On the other hand, Calum wasn't that easy to move, or to dismiss. She might not be able to walk away unaffected from his kiss. She definitely didn't want Calum's kiss.

"Afraid that I might enter your boudoir during the night, Petrovna?" The sensuous masculine challenge wrapped around her. The warm color of night smoke, his eyes traced her body. He smiled lightly at her tall, polished boots.

She braced her legs apart and placed her hands on her hips. Her boots matched anything perfectly, from tight leather miniskirts to long, dynamic dresses. And in a pinch, they were great in mountain snow.

"The day I'm afraid of you, I'll give away my bangle bracelets." He smelled great. That dark, dangerous, mysterious scent, layered with a brisk after-shave. She could easily get used to the sight of him wearing jeans and smelling great. But she could see that he wasn't buying anything. She was losing her touch. She decided to treat him lightly...if she could. Her chin went up a notch. "Are the breakfast croissants ready?"

Calum stared down at her. "Petrovna, give up. Promise me you'll leave Olson alone and we'll call it quits. I'll clean up your trail, and we can both go our own ways."

"How you sweet-talk me, Tallchief. Dream on, big boy. I'll call it quits when I have Olson begging for mercy. I want him to face every life he's ruined." Talia waltzed past him and took the stairs to the kitchen two at a time. Calum was too alert this morning, focused on her. She preferred not to play the mouse to his cat. "Nice house, by the way. Love the light wood contemporary furniture against the dark paneling. Perfect for plants and lots of stuff."

Within the hour, Calum was holding his dozing baby niece close to him and cooing at her. In the midst of a sterile kitchen packed with gadgets, the timeless scene of man and baby caused Talia's heart to do flip-flops. Obviously taken by his niece, Calum leaned against the counter while Sybil, Elspeth and Talia sat at the huge table. The only softening colors in the spacious kitchen were those of the small potted herbs on the window and Elspeth's woven place mats.

The image of a Western cowboy, dressed in worn flannel shirt, shearling vest, jeans and boots, Calum could have posed for a calendar. His four-month-old niece cuddled against him. Megan stirred in his arms, her gray eyes, so like Calum's, finding Talia. Talia barely breathed, aching to hold the baby, yet startled by how much she ached for a child of her own.

Calum's darkened gray gaze met hers, and for a moment Talia's heart stopped. Something caught like gold dust on the sunlight between them. Then she swallowed and wondered if she wasn't catching a flu, and was momentarily weak with it, rather than with the image of a cowboy holding a baby. Calum eased Megan into Sybil's arms and leaned back against the counter, sipping his coffee and studying Talia. She forced her stare away from him; Calum had dangerous edges, and she had just touched one of them.

"It's all in Una's journals." Sybil rocked Megan, who was sleeping on her lap. "She came to this country, an indentured servant, and was captured by Tallchief, a Sioux chieftain. She tamed him, and together they built a life on Tallchief Mountain." She kissed Megan's jet-black hair. "Duncan and his brothers share certain instincts inherited from their great-great-grandfather."

"This plaid is beautiful." Talia, still reeling from the effect Calum had upon her, traced the place mats Elspeth had woven. "This shade of green is marvelous."

"It's the Fearghus plaid, with adjustments. Dragon green for the fierce chieftains of the Sioux and the Fearghuses. I believe my brothers have that same proud fierceness when tested. The vermilion red is to recognize Tallchief. He must have paid dearly to marry a woman not of his blood. He gave up everything for her, and loved her deeply . . . after she tamed him."

"Tell me more about your family." Talia glanced at Calum, who shot Sybil and Elspeth a dark warning look. "Why don't you run along, darlin'?" she asked him, and wondered whether she could tame him. Did she want to?

Did she want to become involved with Calum? She considered the notion, She'd avoided romantic entanglements her entire lifetime. She'd avoided men like Calum, quiet, unpredictable men with shadows and edges. They couldn't be trusted; she'd found that out the day she was to have been married. And after living with the dynamic, emotional Petrovna males, she preferred men who were easily managed and who let her waltz away easily.

He reached for his Western hat and took a deep breath that lifted the hard planes of his chest. "I'll be back for lunch," he stated meaningfully, and shot a dark look at Talia.

She returned it with a kiss tossed into the fragrant air. The muscles in Calum's jaw tensed instantly. Then he nodded to the women sitting at his kitchen table. Talia studied his taut backside and rigid shoulders as he walked out to a pasture where an Arabian stallion gleamed in the morning sun. With the stark Rocky Mountains, tipped in snow, as a backdrop, Calum presented a delicious picture of the cowboy. The black beast whinnied and reared, his front hooves pawing in the air. Then he raced away into the pasture, tail high and flying. In a moment, he raced back to the gate to stand meekly as Calum saddled him.

Calum's efficient movements came from experience. He had lost his city look; he was all rugged Westerner.

Talia hadn't realized she was staring, fascinated by Calum's Western image. His hands soothed the horse, and Talia shivered. When he held Megan, Talia's resolve to lead an independent life had turned to warm butter. The appealing picture of the two Tallchiefs, uncle and baby niece, could make a woman wish for—

Duncan rode up to him on a more heavily built horse, and another, younger version of the Tallchief brothers appeared at Calum's side. They rode toward the huge jutting mountain known as Tallchief.

"Calum and Duncan are so much alike. Yet so different." Elspeth sipped her tea and studied her brothers, sitting tall in the saddle. "Birk is like them, too, despite his lighter side. My three older brothers bore the burden of growing up too soon. They rode off like that when our parents were murdered. The three of them were the only men capable of tracking in the mountains at night. I stayed behind to care for Fiona. I knew they would catch him. My father had taught them well. He'd been taught by his father, and so forth, back to Tallchief. I wanted to go desperately. I did resent not being able to go with them, but they don't know it. In a pinch, I can track as well as they."

Talia touched the small scar on Elspeth's thumb. "That looks like Calum's."

"Aye." Elspeth's tone was gentle, loving, and her eyes were warm. Talia sensed that the Tallchiefs' "Aye" meant that their emotions ran deep. Elspeth continued, tracing the plaid. "There was a night on our mountain, with the fierce October wind howling and Tallchief Lake lashed with white waves. Our parents were lying beneath the cold ground, and we were all afraid. It was Duncan who reached into the night to pluck an idea, a way for us to survive as a family, to keep our heritage."

Elspeth paused, caught by the past, then continued, "When we were very young, the five of us had cut our thumbs and mixed our blood . . . to our mother's horror. She was a passionate woman, in the few times she was angered. I remember her calling out Dad and leveling him for encouraging us. Suddenly he became very romantic. We played with swords and we shouted 'Aye!' as Una's chieftain ancestors had. The Tallchiefs were also quite good at spears and bows and arrows."

Talia ached for the five orphans facing the world, none of them certain about the future. She had been tucked in the safety of the Petrovnas until she managed to escape. Except for visits, she preferred not to stay too long. They were in a family ruled by traditions, and they wanted her safely married, inevitably presenting an array of overbearing potential husbands. She preferred a life without the confinements of marriage.

Elspeth's expression softened. "We each had special names, and we still do—Duncan the defender, Calum the cool, Birk the rogue, Elspeth the elegant and Fiona the fiery. And that night, Duncan called us out to do our best. We raised our scarred thumbs to the sky and pledged that we would survive. That night, we wrapped our heritage around us to keep us safe."

Sybil reached out to touch Elspeth's shoulder. "You used the legends?"

"The legends. Aye..." Soft memories lay in Elspeth's tone. "The legends served to calm our shaking hearts. We were so frightened, and we needed more to survive than our wills. So we clung to what we knew and cherished. The stories written by Una and held dear by our family since. The legends pasted the safety of the past around us. We literally wrapped ourselves in that security."

Elspeth touched Megan's soft black hair, then straightened. Her expression indicated she was looking back into the past. "Una described her dowry, sold to protect Tallchief Mountain. Each item of the Fearghus bridal dowry carried a legend, and we pledged to find an item and return it to our family. We spent our family time discussing it, to lighten the load we all carried. Duncan was to find the cradle, and Sybil brought it to him. The legend came true—*The woman who brings the cradle to a man of Fearghus blood will fill it with his babies*. Calum has pledged to find—"

"The ring," Talia said thoughtfully, interrupting her. "And what was its legend?"

Sybil smiled at Elspeth, who was smoothing a table mat of the Tallchief plaid. "Calum will tell you the legend soon enough. He had paid dearly to keep us together, scraping pennies and paying bills and keeping us afloat. It wasn't easy keeping a growing family in clothes and food. Fiona was just ten when it happened. I was fourteen. My brothers were deathly afraid a well-meaning matron would snatch us from them. It almost killed Fiona to mind her manners, but she did."

"Elspeth, you helped, too. Keeping the house going and your brothers in hand couldn't have been easy." Sybil soothed Megan, who stirred, awakening. The baby opened her gray eyes to stare at Talia.

Talia's heart lurched instantly. She yearned to hold the baby, to cuddle her. She shivered, unused to her maternal instincts surfacing. She wrapped her arms around herself protectively. She didn't want the warmth of this family, or the enchantment of this small town, with its freshly baked pies and laughing children.

She wanted nothing of Calum's to enfold her, to fascinate her.

She wanted freedom, and mornings without great-looking, great-smelling, sultry, gray-eyed cowboys. "Tell me about Tallchief's stone, the one Calum wears."

"That was the first stone Una threw at Tallchief. It wasn't her last. She was just as proud as he was. In the end, they loved each other. Would you like to hold Megan?" Elspeth asked softly. Then Sybil was placing the warm child within Talia's arms. A tiny hand gripped Talia's pinkie while Megan watched her steadily.

Talia swallowed and moved her little finger, enchanted with Megan. She looked up to see Sybil and Elspeth smiling softly. "Aye," Elspeth said.

"Aye," Sybil returned.

"My brother has already taken you to his cabin, hasn't he?" Elspeth asked.

"Yes. We, ah . . . needed a break in the drive," Talia answered, distracted by Megan's cooing. She found herself cooing back, something she had never done.

Megan clasped Talia's single braid and took her heart.

Later, when Sybil and Elspeth were gone, Talia called her mother, assuring her that she was safe. Her mother promised to send her clothing and, with a smile in her voice, told Talia to stay out of trouble. Then Talia called Marco the Fence and asked him to contact Vinnie and Nose for a lead on the ring. Marco the Fence promised to get back to her.

After a quick search of the kitchen, Talia found the grocery's telephone number. The clerk seemed stunned when she placed a delivery order. "A woman in Calum Tallchief's house? You bet. We'll have this delivery over there in no time. Oh, sure. We have watercress.... Er...uh...we'll send someone down to the creek for fresh-grown. I can't believe it. Calum brought home a woman. Hey, lady, are you the one with the red sports car hooked to the back of his rig?"

"I am. I'm his new housekeeper. My car seems to be missing its distributor cap. I'd love to locate a new one before win-

ter settles in. I hope you have a wonderful fish market
here—'' Talia frowned as the clerk's snickers became roaring
laughter, apparently shared by the other customers.

The groceries arrived within half an hour, and the delivery-
man never stopped grinning. "Hot dog. Calum brought home
a woman," he exclaimed as she signed the bill.

"Is that a novelty?"

"Huh? Oh, no, ma'am. Brings 'em home all the time. Herds
of them. Tall...short...all kinds. Lots of women," the clerk
answered, and chuckled as he closed the door behind him. He
motioned to a passing truck and ran out onto the road. Several pickup trucks stopped, with the drivers looking and
pointing and grinning at Calum's house. Then the sheriff's
patrol car passed by with the emotionally charged music of an
Italian opera, and the small convention dispersed instantly.

Talia packed away the groceries, then explored Calum's
home. Of wood and stone, the house was sleek and func-
tional, revealing little about the man. Elspeth's weaving perfectly tempered the sterile browns and creams. Upstairs,
Calum's closets and dresser were neat; in a framed picture, a
younger, happier Calum held a beautiful woman dressed in a
wedding gown against him. A small pain shot through Talia's
heart; Calum had loved deeply. She ached for all the bright
expectations of the groom, and for the hardened man Calum
was now. There was no denying the blatant sexuality of the
blue-eyed, black-haired woman. She had a haunting face and
a lush body that curved intimately against Calum's. The faces
in the photograph smiled at Talia, making her uneasy. The
woman and Calum had already been lovers, and judging by the
way the woman's hand rested possessively on Calum's flat
stomach, she'd wanted him then.

Talia's fingers shook as she replaced the photograph. She
didn't want to know Calum's secrets or sense the heat running between the people in the photograph. She closed her eyes
and placed her hands over her stomach. Calum still loved the
woman, keeping the photograph when nothing else feminine
remained in the house. His private bathroom bore his scent, his
shaving gear neatly arranged. She leaned against the wall,
stunned by her sudden need to see him. Unused to needing

anyone, to a sense of homecoming, Talia shook her head. She wouldn't have Calum affecting her, deterring her from her revenge. Nor did she want to realize the torrid sexuality of his past.

She bit her lip. She'd never been jealous, but now there was no denying the hot crush of it. Just that much more reason to run like the very devil from him . . .

She picked the lock of another room and entered the shadows of a different century. A bow and a beaded, fringed quiver of arrows hung on the wall with a brilliantly colored war shield. A large wooden bowl was filled with balls of homespun yarn. Carved wooden spoons and trenchers lay beside it. A length of Tallchief plaid lay tossed aside, and Talia held it high. The kilt would look gorgeous with the man's ruffled shirt hanging on the wall.

Elspeth's weaving was beautiful. Talia studied the plaid and then laid it aside. She lifted the cuff of the shirt to her nose. Calum's scent swirled around her, a mixture of soap and male.

She moved through the shadows, touching what was evidently very dear to Calum Tallchief. A huge old knife gleamed, stuck deep in a weathered board bearing the Tallchief brand, a stick man and a mountain.

A blanket of Native American design covered an old, comfortable couch, out of place in Calum's modern home.

Another wooden bowl, full of amulets and beads, gleamed in the dim light. Drawn to it, Talia lifted a delicately crafted necklace of blue and red beads.

A folded pale doeskin vest, exquisite with beaded flowers and fringes, lay soft beneath her fingers. Talia touched old ledgers, the books worn, yet obviously treasured. She lifted a framed photograph of the Tallchief family. The adult Tallchiefs looked at each other with love, their happy brood cuddled against them. Talia's fingertip traced Calum, already wearing glasses. He'd been a bright-looking, angular boy, his happy expression bearing no resemblance to the man he was now. Talia mourned the shadows of his life.

The door opened slowly, and Calum filled it, a broad-shouldered Western male with his legs spread in a showdown stance. Talia swallowed, and a little warning trickle of fear shot up her spine. "Can I help you find anything?" he asked, too softly, as he removed his glasses.

His face was shadowed, yet there was no mistaking the set of his shoulders as he walked toward her. She realized instantly that she had found his deepest center, his heart's lair, where he was vulnerable and yet protective of what was his. The lifting of the hair on her nape told her that Calum considered everything in this room his, including her. There was no mistaking the purpose of the graceful male moving toward her. She would pay for entering his privacy. Talia backed against the wall and tried to paste a fearless expression on her face. "Home so soon, darlin'? Gee, that's a great kilt. I bet you'd look marvy—"

One of Calum's big hands flattened on the wall beside her, and the other wrapped gently around the nape of her neck. His thumb began to move slowly, caressing her skin. His voice was too soft. "Your heart is beating like a frightened rabbit's. Are you afraid of me, of being caught here?"

"Get . . . back . . ."

Talia flattened against the wall. Close to her, Calum was too big, too powerful, and too dangerous. She'd always loved a good challenge, and that was what all six feet four inches of Calum Tallchief offered. She could meet him any day, on any plane. "Move, Tallchief."

"When I'm ready."

She wasn't waiting. She pushed hard against his stomach and found it unrelenting. Calum's hand slid from her neck to her back, and flattened her against him, in a movement so quick she couldn't protest. "Lady, you are nothing but trouble."

She'd never been possessed, held so tightly that her heart beat against a man's. Instantly her body dismissed the clothing between them, her hunger and fascination startling her. Something dark, fierce and primitive stilled and heated the air between them. Then Calum moved, and Talia found herself tumbling onto the spacious woven couch.

In the shadows, he lay over her, his weight confining but not hurting. Fascinated by the shadows of his face, by the heat burning between them, Talia managed to breathe as his gaze swept her mouth and lingered on her throat.

A taker, she thought distantly. A man who would not be denied. Nor would she.

He had not hurt her; he waited for her to answer the sensations running hotly, tautly between them. Calum was controlled now, waiting for her permission. He would leave her—if she wanted. He'd given her a choice.

Softness shifted within her, answering, soothing, wanting. She fought the need of her hips to lift to him, and feared the demand of his body against hers. Talia lowered her lashes to shield her emotions. The position was too intimate, too demanding, and Calum suited too well the role of the dominant male possessing a woman he wanted.

Her heart lurched wildly. She'd lived her life with excitement and sometimes danger, but Calum represented a feast of both. She would take this moment. She placed her hands on his shoulders and gripped him.

His eyes held hers as his hand moved slowly to cover her breast, to enclose the unbound softness, gently, firmly. He sucked in his breath, and she trembled. Or was it him?

His hand rested upon her possessively, not moving, not hurting. "You're frightened, aren't you?"

"I'm not afraid of anything, Tallchief," she managed, in a voice that was too soft and husky to be threatening. Her fingers pressed into his shoulders, yet did not force him away. She caught her breath as his hand opened, his fingertips smoothing her skin.

Slowly his eyes lowered upon her body.

Unable to deny herself, Talia looked to where her black sweater had come free from its buttons. To where his hand covered her bare breast.

There in the shadows, she watched his thumb move slowly across her nipple, peaking it.

Unable to look away, Talia met the glitter of his gray eyes. "You're heavy, you know."

"Am I? Are you uncomfortable? Why are you shaking?" Though his tone seemed almost clinical, hot steel flashed in his eyes.

"That's you, Tallchief."

He shifted between her legs, only layers of denim separating his desire from her. "Petrovna, you're burning like a furnace. If I put my mouth on that fine white skin, you'll ignite."

Her breath caught. She fought the need to grasp his arrogant black head and bring it to her breast. Her fingers fluttered upon his taut shoulders.

"Your eyes are huge. What do you want me to do?" His voice was deep, mysterious, fascinating. "This?"

He slowly eased aside her sweater to caress her other breast. She cried out, arching to his touch and thoroughly shocking herself. Then, with a moan, she locked her arms around his neck and tugged at him.

Calum didn't budge. "You're used to having things your way, Petrovna. Not this time. After what I've been through with you, I like having you under me and obedient."

"*Obedient?* Don't you dare think for one minute that you can use sex—"

Calum slowly lowered his head and took her mouth. He tasted of everything she wanted—passion, mystery, heat, storms.... She allowed his tongue to enter her lips, taking up the fascinating rhythm with her own. Then he began to nibble on her bottom lip, tugging on it. He bit gently on her earlobe, his breath swirling warmly, roughly, upon her skin.

His kiss tormented, possessed, teased, lingered and took. She was vaguely aware of the purring deep in her throat. Her legs moved along his, allowing him deeper into the cradle of her body. She thought she heard him murmur, "Jasmine and silk," and then she gasped as his hot face fitted against her throat, his kisses over her skin leaving heat as they passed.

His open lips found her aching breast, tugged at it, and she cried out softly again, sensitive to the erotic suckling. Calum's hand moved down her body, cupping her hips, lifting her to him. There was a movement at her waist, and she gasped as his warm hand flattened possessively on her bare stomach. "Calum..."

She bit his throat—a slight, instinctive nibble—because he tasted so good.

The sound running through his throat pleased her, a rough, deep yearning.

She almost cried out as his fingers found her, stroked her, warmed her into flowing, melting honey. She held him tightly and gave, moving her hips higher, undulating and lifting herself to his touch. Calum's breath caught, and his hand gently eased away. "What are you doing?" she managed when he lifted his head, looking down at her with an amused tenderness.

"You're very tight, Petrovna. Chances are you're a damned hot, wet, eager, jasmine-scented virgin. I might have known you couldn't be trusted to play fair." Yet Calum's voice was soft, his lips moving across the tears on her cheeks.

"I might not be," she threw back at him in her defense. "But thanks for the anatomy lesson, anyway." She wished she wasn't shaking violently and that he wasn't wearing a beguiling, pleased masculine smile. Trust a man like this one, a methodical, low-down, no-good expert kisser to discover she hadn't been—

"So, despite all your accomplishments, you haven't been touched. And you ignite when my mouth is on you."

"I do not. I was faking. You are terribly out-of-date. Everyone knows that men like that sort of thing. At least in my experience, they do." She ached horribly from the need to have him touch her. Tears burned her eyes. She realized with horror that she was shaking fiercely. "Don't you kiss me, Tallchief. I despise you. I'd rather kiss Godzilla with two heads."

"You like kissing me, Petrovna. Admit it." He chuckled; it was a disarming sound. Then he shifted, drawing her to his side, and placed her head upon his chest. Talia wished that she hadn't cuddled instinctively closer to his hard body, that her leg hadn't ensnared his and that her arm hadn't wrapped around his waist. He wasn't going anywhere just yet. She wasn't ready to release him. Beneath her cheek, she could hear Calum's heart racing.

He stroked her temple, and rocked her against him. She felt a little as Megan must have, warm and safe and cherished. "Better?" he asked in a tender tone that disarmed her.

She wouldn't admit her needs, not if he poured honey on her and placed her on an anthill. But she wouldn't let him go, either. She flattened her hand on his chest and traced the breadth slowly. She traced Tallchief's stone, a part of Calum's inheritance. Beneath the worn flannel shirt, his nipples peaked against her palm. She slowly moved her palm again, fascinated by the hard nubs. Calum sucked in his breath as she moved her hand downward.

She wanted to touch him. To enfold his strength in her hand and explore— He caught her wrist and drew her hand to his lips. "Don't."

Talia stared at him. She scrambled over Calum, pausing as a big hand smoothed her bottom in a caress. Then she made the mistake of looking back at him.

He sprawled there in the shadows, all delicious male, a grin on his face. She blinked at the tenderness and the soft invitation in his voice. "Come here, Petrovna. You're shaking in your boots."

The hair on the nape of her neck lifted. She glanced down his hard body to find his jeans very tight across his hips. His blatant sexuality frightened her. Or was it herself and her need to feast upon him? She'd never let a man come so close to her, touch her, place his mouth upon her and tear the very hunger from her femininity. Talia blinked. Calum was very pleased with himself, this arrogant, sexy, all-dynamite male that she couldn't possibly have let— She backed up and gripped a ball of yarn. For once she didn't trust herself. She pelted him with yarn balls as he slowly rose, his shirt opened by her fingers, and walked to her.

Talia, who never blushed, found that her face was hot. She eased back into the shadows, hoping he wouldn't notice. Calum very gently buttoned her sweater, and the sweetness of the gesture almost caused her tears to return. "What's for lunch?" he asked gently.

She sniffed, uncertain and wary and not pleased about the blush running hotly down her body. Calum wasn't playing by her rules. She'd have to find that darn ring and free herself. Olson needed— "Lunch?"

He smoothed a strand of hair across his hand and wrapped it around his finger, studying the shades. "You're the housekeeper, remember? You're supposed to cook for me."

"Listen, you jerk. I have never liked the idea of me Tarzan, you Jane—"

He ran his thumb over her thick braid and drew it to her breast. His fingertips grazed her flushed cheek. "Wear a bra from now on, Petrovna. My brothers will be here shortly. Birk is unmarried and looking."

She lifted her chin. She didn't want to be enchanted by Calum's hot sultry look. No man had a right to be that enticing. "You just can't trust nerds to be what they're supposed to be anymore," she stated haughtily, before walking out of the room on unsteady legs.

Behind her, Calum stated softly, "Petrovna, you've got a bad habit of wanting the last word. I find that a challenge."

She sensed then, with a trickle of fear, that Duncan Tallchief wasn't the only Tallchief male with possessive carry-woman-home tendencies.

Calum placed a boot on his fireplace and surveyed his ruined kingdom. He glanced at his previously uncluttered living room, where boxes of Talia's clothing had been opened and scattered everywhere. Emily, Duncan's stepdaughter, had arrived with her kittens, now playing amid a stack of frothy lace lingerie. A red lace teddy had been tossed on one of his lamps, and a huge chest of costume jewelry, all of which made noise, was open. Talia had screamed with delight when her things arrived, and, fascinated, Calum had stood back to watch her rip open the boxes and tear out the colorful clothing.

She enchanted him, a woman who seemed worldly-wise but who'd blushed furiously, her eyes huge, when he approached her upstairs. He'd found her in the midst of everything that was dear to him, and his instincts had told him that she belonged to him, that she was his and where she should be. His first impulse had been to lay her down and make love to her amid the treasures of his family, his life.

He wanted to be in her, to be captured by her warmth, held close and—

Calum's entire body ached to claim Talia's and to cherish her. The knowledge rocked everything that was safe within him, the barriers that he had placed around his heart.

He was still shaken by her virginity. She'd ignited under him, and the feel of her skin beneath his mouth would torture him for hours. The movement of her hips arching up to his touch could drive a man insane— Her blush had sent him walking on air.

Later, at his kitchen table, Duncan and Birk were eyeing tiny watercress-and-cucumber sandwiches. Emily had run all the way from school, stopping only to pick up her kittens, to meet Calum's guest. She'd arrived breathless, with a carload of boys following her. Duncan, Birk and Calum had immediately gone to the porch and glared at the boys, to Emily's horror.

Talia carefully ladled asparagus soup into bowls; it was uncommon fare in beef-and-potatoes Amen Flats. Dressed in a hot-pink top tied in a knot beneath her breasts and a long sarong-style skirt over skintight pants, Talia added basil sprigs to the platter of tiny sandwiches. Her artistic flourishes caused her bangle bracelets to jingle. The crystal drops flowing from her ears caught the sun and lit her skin. Calum scowled at the length of straight blond hair swaying down to her waist as she moved. He found himself staring at the undulating sway of her hips. No woman should move with that sensuality.

Talia caught his glare and tossed him a challenging smile. She patted him on the top of the head as she passed to sit by Birk.

Emily grinned up at Duncan as he frowned at the soup. The teenager touched the rhinestone beauty-queen tiara on her head, evidence of Talia's jaunt in the glamorous world of the pageant runway. "Eat up, Dad. It's just good old everyday asparagus soup."

Fresh in from taking cattle to a lower pasture on Tallchief Mountain, Duncan and Birk eyed the tiny sandwiches suspiciously. "Grass," Duncan stated finally, after probing the watercress.

"She's a gourmet cook. Took classes in France. Burned up a top chef's kitchen. He went into a sanitorium to recuperate." Calum's body vibrated with the need to take Talia. Every time she came close, he caught the scent of jasmine that arose from her skin. He wanted to order everyone out and kiss Talia until she melted.

He wanted those soft lips on his. She'd just thrown him a curve, and he was still reeling from his emotions. He began to feel the weight of Alek's and Papa Petrovna's concern. Despite Talia's sexy look and adventures, she had no idea what an aroused male could do.

Calum frowned at the tiny watercress sandwich. He resented her threat to his life and his control and his reputation. He understood the chef's lawsuit against the cooking school for letting Talia into his class.

Talia shrugged, and her bangles tinkled. "André wanted more flames in my cherries jubilee. I gave them to him. I couldn't help it if the curtains ignited. You know, I'd love to do a really good bouillabaisse with French bread. Is there a good fish market here?"

"Ma'am, I'd be happy to take you fishing. Tallchief Lake offers some of the best there is." Birk's grin widened, and for the first time, the keen edge of jealousy pricked Calum.

"*I'll* take her." Calum eased the delicious asparagus soup into his mouth and tried not to look at the woman who had folded gracefully to the floor to cuddle a kitten. Calum had compromised his reputation, linked up with a woman who acted like a temptress but whose body had never been touched, and had just agreed to spend his afternoon fishing, when he should have been tearing out her secrets. Talia nuzzled the kitten, and Calum felt himself go weak. Alek Petrovna would skin him alive if anything happened to her. Talia was set on ruining Olson, who was probably very experienced at forcing and blackmailing women.

Calum's house was infested with Tallchief men, an array of sexy and colorful clothing, a woman who wanted to cook bouillabaisse in beef-eating rural Wyoming...and a younger brother who was leering at Talia— Calum wanted to pick her up and run to his favorite spot on Tallchief Mountain. He scowled at Elspeth's woven place mat. An action like that—carrying off Talia—would prove she had gotten to him. He was a controlled man, a logical man. He did not allow his emotions to rule him.

Calum looked up to see Duncan grinning broadly at him. "Find that ring yet?" Duncan asked.

"I will," Talia said confidently as she stroked the kitten on her lap. "I'd love to hear the legend attached to it."

"He didn't tell you? Mmm... That's why we call him Calum the cool. Has to do with—" Birk began, then closed his lips when Duncan lifted a warning eyebrow.

Calum stared at her and noted the slightly swollen curve of her lips caused by his kisses. *When a man of Fearghus blood places the ring upon the right woman's finger, he'll capture his true love forever.*

Without thinking about the consequences of his next move, Calum stood. He placed his hat on his head, then grabbed a warm jacket and stuffed Talia into it. He stooped to pluck her up and place her across his shoulder. He walked out the door, carrying a startled, indignant woman. Duncan's and Birk's laughter followed him. They stood at the door, grinning, as he placed her on his Arabian stallion and swung up in front of her. Birk came at a run, bearing Calum's extra jeans, a bag of collapsible fishing poles and a tackle box. He tossed the jeans to Talia and swung the bag over the saddle horn. "You might need this, brother."

"He's going to need more than that. You can't just sling me over your shoulder like that. I am not a sack of potatoes," Talia stated warningly.

"I'll say," Birk returned appreciatively with a grin.

"Dibs." Calum heard himself mutter the Tallchiefs' boyhood term for possession. He disliked the unstable emotions coursing through him and the knowledge that Duncan had claimed Sybil, using the same word. The woman seated behind him wearing a filmy skirt, body-molding pants and tall black leather boots would make any man act irrationally. Calum realized that he had just placed his hand, gloved in rough work leather, possessively upon her knee. Talia had very nice knees.

"Hey, Birk!" Duncan called from the steps. He wrapped his arm around Emily, at his side. "Lacey just called. She wants you to know that she's bought all the roofing nails in Amen Flats. She hopes you won't be late on that roofing contract."

Birk's grin died. He scowled and stalked toward his horse.

"What's that about?" Talia asked, holding her breath as Birk raced his horse for a fence and cleared it beautifully.

"Don't ask. Lacey MacCandliss and Birk have been warring for years. She's a builder, and his competition." Calum stopped talking.

Talia smiled behind his back. "Gotcha. You almost told me something I wanted to know. You could make this all easier if you'd tell me everything I want to know and if you'd let me find that ring and if you'd trade me Olson for it. As my accomplice, I'd think you'd want to make things easy for me."

Calum turned slightly, looking over his shoulder, down at her. His expression told her that nothing would be easy with Calum Tallchief. She'd have to fight him every step of the way. He lifted one thick black brow, then turned around, leaving her with his broad back.

Talia smiled and wrapped her arms around him. She leaned her cheek against his back and cuddled close to his warmth. There was just something old-fashioned and sweet about the way he'd plucked her from the midst of his family. This man had touched her intimately—because she'd let him—and she wallowed in the thought that she had shocked him. "Did you love her?" she asked, her heart stopping as she waited for his answer.

His answer took a long time. She sensed him considering the past when he returned, "She's never been in my house. She hated the country." Calum's answer snapped back to her on the chilling wind.

She slid her hand inside his jacket and found the stone. He allowed the trespass, and she snuggled closer, surprised that she wanted to soothe him and wrap him safely in her arms. "Then ... you never took her to your cabin, either, right?"

She edged higher, and watched, fascinated, as Calum's cheek flushed. "Shut up, Petrovna," he murmured easily, and pressed her hand to the stone.

Her heart did a happy little flip-flop. "You know, Tallchief? I'm getting to you. I'll have you right in the palm of my hand before you know it."

Five

―――――

"Calum yells? I thought Birk was the only Tallchief male who did that." Lacey MacCandliss grinned over the mug of "brewski" with which she had just toasted Talia. It was Tuesday, ladies' night at Maddy's Hot Spot. Sybil, Elspeth, Lacey and Talia were sharing a table, upon which Maddy had placed a vase of battered silk roses. The forgotten price tag on one dusty rose trembled when Lacey removed her battered work boots from the table and her chair hit the floor.

Talia continued her story. "All I was doing was standing on a log and rolling it on the water to angle for a better place to fish. I just happened to be holding the stringer of fish we'd caught, and when he yelled, it slipped from my hand. I'm an expert logroller...learned how in Canada...the lumberjacks were only too happy to teach me. Calum didn't have to dive into the lake and push me to safety. He could have unbalanced me, and that water is so cold. When I was ready, I could have simply walked the log back to shore. When we rode back to the house, I couldn't tell if his teeth were gritting or chattering. I hope he doesn't catch cold. He is in a foul and evil mood, for some reason.''

Talia smiled to herself. Though she had been terrified when Calum dived into the water, he had responded magnificently to her administrations when they arrived home. For a moment, she'd thought that he might tug her into his hot, steaming shower. The thought had appealed; Calum, she had learned, was a very sensual man, and one who touched carefully, gently. She would have trusted him to take her into his keeping; she'd wanted him desperately, wanted to hold him and soothe the pain that she sensed lurking near his leashed emotions. Then he'd muttered something to himself and firmly closed the door. He had glared at her and muttered again when she made him lunch—this time with a dark, menacing tone—but had drunk every drop of her chicken soup. She was getting to him. No doubt about it.

Talia grinned at Lacey, who had come soaring up to Calum's house on her big black motorcycle. With a getaway driver at hand and a chance to nettle Calum, Talia had hitched up her tiny black skirt and hopped on the back. Ladies' night at Maddy's was just what she needed. Maddy, the beefy bartender-owner, served lemonade, nonalcoholic beer, and drinks for those who wanted them. A former pro football player, he had covered the pictures of naked ladies with sheets and had saturated the tavern with flowery air freshener in honor of the female customers. He wore a black T-shirt without holes, and a bow tie. A lemon sucker replaced his usual cigar. Patty Jo Black, a sizable farm wife with a steamy voice dipped in rhythm and blues, played rock and roll on the piano.

A big banner, painted by a ranch wife with five children, was spread across the mirror Maddy protected in every fight. The banner read No garden planting, childbirth, or Intelligent and Beautiful Children stories allowed. The ladies of Amen Flats relaxed, teased each other about the latest hunk's taut backside, discussed soap operas and relaxed around the tavern. Sybil, dressed in a classic gray cardigan set and slacks, smiled at Talia. ''Duncan yells sometimes—I just thought I'd share that. It's really quite lovely when he does. I find a good out-

and-out battle invigorating at times—he's usually so controlled.''

Elspeth shook her head. ''My brothers never yelled while we were fighting to stay together. Those times were grim, with the child authorities wanting to take away everyone but Duncan. He was just eighteen, and took legal responsibility for all of us. We had family friends, but we were so frightened back then. I remember Calum working all night at accounts—juggling them—until a couple hours before the school bus arrived and then going to school. Even in our darkest times, they quietly shielded us, and they never raised their voices.''

Sybil's sleek, knotted hair gleamed like rich copper as she leaned closer; a faint sprinkle of freckles dusted her nose. Sybil had had her own dark times. She understood fear, and to lighten the moment she shared a secret about Duncan. ''The thing that Duncan does even better than the Tallchief kiss is roar magnificently. He looks so horrified when he's discovered he's yelled. Poor baby. Since Emily has turned fifteen and is wanting to date, he's really been distracted. His brothers have joined him in protecting her against marauding teenage boys.''

''The Tallchief kiss?'' Talia remembered Calum's mouth tormenting, teasing hers, fascinating her into a dark, stormy world heated by the pulse of her own heartbeat.

''They should bottle it.'' Sybil grinned. ''The first time Duncan kissed me, I—'' She flushed elegantly. ''Actually, he's quite...passionate.'' Her blush deepened.

Elspeth snorted delicately. ''Surviving as a teenage girl who wanted to date wasn't easy in our family. My brothers frightened every male in the territory. The three of them would just stand there, thumbs hooked in their belts, legs spread like gunfighters, and stare. That's all it took. A simple Tallchief staredown, and the boys ran for safety. Fiona and I were outraged.''

Sybil grinned. ''That's exactly what they do. Look deadly, when they're really just big pushover pussycats. They're perfect with Emily, except when it comes to her growing up and dating. She loves them, but is planning revenge with a party at our house. Duncan is chaperoning. Birk is to assist. I believe

Calum's last crime was plucking a prime candidate right from her pucker. She thinks Talia is a great payback.''

"Moi?" Talia lifted her eyebrows innocently. She liked these women and their warmth. Lacey was a recognized member of the family. With short black curly hair and a height well under the Tallchiefs', Lacey was quick to grin, yet elements of sadness lay beneath her surface.

Lacey glanced outside Maddy's tavern to the well-lit street. "Calum's four-wheeler is out there. I see three heads, probably Duncan and Birk with him. Emily is staying overnight at a friend's, but Duncan probably has Megan with him—they're starting the car, probably to warm it up. Ladies' night at Maddy's has always driven Birk nuts. He can't stand the thought of women being holed up without him. He is so disgusting around women, such a flirt. But Calum surprises me. I never heard of an employer keeping such close tabs on his housekeeper.''

Elspeth shook her head. "I was hoping no one would notice them. Megan is having a wonderful time out there with the three of them doting on her. They're probably doing some bop-shoo-wop song for her right now. No doubt my brothers are overheated while Megan is perfectly comfortable. They're probably discussing how silly it is to have a baby out on an October night.''

Talia glanced at her. "You seem to have a sixth sense regarding your family.''

"It's a shaman thing, and maybe a bit from Una Fearghus's Celtic ancestors,'' Lacey offered. "Elspeth feels it sometimes about me.'' She met Elspeth's quiet gaze. "Like the time Elspeth knew my mother— Well, my mother wasn't a happy woman, and she took it out on me. Elspeth told her mother. I never saw Pauline Tallchief in a high temper but once, and that was when she called my mother out. That was what she did—called her out and promised her, not threatened her, but promised my mother what she would do to her if anything happened to me. I never saw my mother so scared as when she saw Pauline Tallchief.''

Lacey traced the top of her beer mug thoughtfully. "I grew up eating more at the Tallchief table and being protected by them than in my own home. Pauline rocked me on her lap as though I was one of her own, and took care of me when I was sick, too. They all did. At school, the Tallchiefs were right there when things got bad for me.''

Elspeth's hand rested on Lacey's. ''We've always loved you.''

Talia caught the tears shimmering in Lacey's eyes before she turned away. Lacey shielded her pain well. She glanced at Talia. ''Elspeth made me a kilt, just like the rest of her family. You should see the three Tallchief brothers dressed up in kilts and ruffled shirts . . . all dark and dangerous and snarling at the world because of it. But they do it because it means so much to Elspeth. Darn near takes my breath away. Put Elspeth into the picture and it's worth a tear. So tell me, Talia, how did you meet Calum?''

Talia flicked a silk rose petal. She wasn't looking forward to another night in Calum's house. After Calum's devastating warm, slow kisses, and his gentle hands treasuring her, heating her body, she'd remained one big blush. She didn't like him knowing that she wasn't all that worldly. She glanced at the women, saw their strength and decided that they would understand. She told them the truth about Olson's sexual harassment of January, and how he had destroyed her happiness, and other women's as well. How Calum had prowled through her crimes and wanted her to ignore her revenge.

''Men,'' Sybil muttered darkly.

''They don't understand,'' Elspeth stated gently, but her gray eyes had a steely glint that reminded Talia of Calum's concealed temper. ''He shouldn't have interfered. You were doing a marvelous job.''

''I agree with you, Talia. You were taking the only course to really teach Olson a lesson and protect other women from the same fate. Olson's downfall definitely needs a feminine touch.'' Sybil glanced toward the street. ''Sometimes Tallchief men are so protective of us that they forget we have needs of our own—a sisterhood thing. I thought Duncan would explode when he discovered that Elspeth and I were . . . well, keeping tabs on our own sleazeball here in Amen Flats. It was nothing more than a few documented accounts of Sleazy's visits, with some excellent night photography involved.''

"Duncan was worried when you went on a stakeout in that field with the buffalo. But it is important to help another woman on a level that does her the most good,'' Elspeth added.

"I'm for it. As a kid, I went through things with sleazes like Olson—men my mother brought home. Sometimes they need more than a legal slap or a thinning of their pocketbooks. They need something potent enough to shake their slimy guts and put fear in them. Any way I can help?''

Talia sat very straight and smiled primly. "Actually, there is.'' She flicked a mischievous glance at Elspeth. "I really wouldn't want to cause the Tallchief family problems, but I do have a debt of honor to complete my mission.''

Elspeth glanced toward the men sitting outside in the vehicle. She tilted her head slightly and studied the roses. "Good. Birk and Duncan are leaving. Duncan is afraid that Calum's sneezing will make Megan catch cold.... You're going after Una's ring, and you want to trade it for a release from Calum. You want to finish the job you started, with no interference from him.'' Elspeth lifted one sleek, questioning eyebrow at Talia.

"You guessed it. Petrovna's Law. We always finish what we start.''

For an instant, Elspeth's fine black brows drew together, her gray eyes darkened as though remembering something unpleasant. "Does you brother, Alek, always finish what he starts?''

"Petrovna's Law,'' Talia stated firmly with a nod.

"Has anyone ever finished anything for him?'' The steely edge in Elspeth's soft voice startled the other women.

Lacey recovered with a quick grin, nodding toward a well-built male at a nearby table. "I'd like to finish plenty with him. Nice buns.''

Sybil, Elspeth and Lacey looked at each other. They began to grin. "Shall we tell her the legend of the ring?'' Sybil asked.

"Not just yet. I really think that is Calum's place,'' Elspeth murmured, her eyes lighting.

"Yeah. Let her find out on her own," Lacey said with a cheeky grin. She dangled the key to an aged commuter plane. "Will this help? If you can manage a takeoff from a paved country road. I borrowed it from a client to scoop all the roofing nails from the nearest towns. Then I called Birk's logical shipping supplier and anonymously questioned his credit. Birk wasn't happy."

Five days later, Calum lowered a small, sleek jet into position. He placed the landing pattern between the two rows of torches on the desert. Prince Kadar Abd al Jabbar's men stood beside the fine blooded Arabian horses, calming them as the plane dipped neatly through the night onto the runway. As Calum taxied to a stop, the desert night spread out upon the endless sands of the small, primitive country, far from civilization.

Calum resented his anger, a gift from Talia. When he first discovered Talia had come here, terror had gripped him. Anything could happen to her. Gradually he'd worked his way through fear to anger. He preferred anger when dealing with Talia; it was safer. He was letting his emotions show. Talia's latest escapade was too dangerous, far more so than Olson's blackmail. He hadn't discovered her getaway until Wednesday night. He'd forgotten how effective Elspeth could be as an accomplice when she set her mind to it. Disguised as Talia, Elspeth had walked to his home while Talia borrowed Lacey's motorcycle and commuter plane.

Calum hadn't had an old-fashioned cold since childhood, but he had one now, thanks to Talia's logrolling incident. When Calum's bad mood and temperature rose, Elspeth had felt obliged to explain that Talia had gone after the ring. Four days of headaches, fever and sneezing had primed Calum for his personal revenge on Talia Petrovna.

Calum regretted the language he'd used on Marco, Nose and Vinnie as he tracked Talia by telephone and sipped his hot lemonade remedy. Alek Petrovna's yelling hadn't helped Calum's headache or anger. The Petrovnas were emotional people, and multilingual. Calum didn't want to know how the Russian threats translated, he just wanted to get his hands on

Talia. She had entered a world where women were still considered chattel, despite Kadar's firm hand in changing his small country.

From a bed laden with tissues and aspirin, Calum had managed to pacify Olson and track Talia. She'd made contact with Marco, Vinnie and Nose. Vinnie had sold a ring answering the description of Una's to a sheikh at the Denver airport. The sheikh had been en route to Cairo, then to his small, primitive kingdom nearby. Talia had impersonated a stewardess, traveled to Cairo and jumped the next camel train to follow the suspect sheikh. After Calum's call, Kadar had simply located her and purchased her.

Kadar welcomed Calum as he stepped from the plane. "My friend! So you have come to claim your butterfly, no?" He hugged Calum warmly, then motioned to his man, who slid a billowing cloak around Calum's shoulders and adjusted a flowing headdress around his head.

The sand, blown by the fierce wind, stung his face, and Calum expertly tucked a portion of the headdress across his face. "Kadar, I thank you."

Kadar chuckled and nodded graciously, in the custom of his country. "Your tone is that of the frustrated hunter. True, the woman is maddening and skilled in almost anything, especially disguises. After so many women hunting you, it pleases me that you have met your match. I have followed your instructions. She is being prepared now by the women of my tribe. They only consented to leave their luxuries and homes to play the nomads of their ancestry because I told them of your love for the woman and how she flees you. In the name of romance, they help you, but also mourn that it is not one of them you wish as a bride. Or a love slave. So this one you want enough to come after her, to keep her safe, no? This is the first woman that I can remember who causes the fire to come to your eyes. Maybe to your heart, eh, old friend?"

In his native robes and poised in the desert night, Kadar looked like a sheikh of his ancestry. Actually, he was a modern man, infuriated by the age-old status of women in his country. As a ruler and politician, he battled to protect his country and to bring it into the contemporary world. Together Kadar and Calum had fought terrorists and slave traders, and Kadar's thumb bore the Tallchief scar. Calum grinned. "Fiona is fine."

While skiing in a Swiss resort, Calum had saved Kadar's sister from an avalanche. Kadar had instantly invited Calum and Fiona—both were on vacation—to visit his palace, and Fiona had caused trouble from the first moment.

Kadar snorted. "That one in there with the evil temper. She almost caused a revolt when you brought her to my palace. Nor is this woman gentle. My bodyguard is sulking back at the palace. She has bested him in wrestling. Is that Russian she curses in so fluently?"

"Among other things. She likes to revert to Apache threats of ants and honey."

Kadar frowned thoughtfully at Calum as they walked to their horses. "If you call for help, we shall both be embarrassed. You know, my friend, I have never seen you so emotional. Do not snort so, you will frighten the horses. I think you are like the stallion catching the scent of the mare, no?"

Talia tugged the tiny beaded bodice downward. The red silk garment was tight, and cut very low to emphasize her breasts. She jingled when she moved, because of the bells on the filmy gold-and-red harem pants. The distance between the bodice and the off-the-hip harem pants showed a smooth expanse of her waist. The golden rings on her toes glistened in the light of the lamps scattered around the elaborate tent. She shook her head, and the string of pearls across her forehead quivered. The tribe was quiet now, and she was left with two hulking bodyguards who watched her closely. An elaborate feast had been prepared by the women flowing through the massive tent. Above their veils, their sloe eyes watched her curiously. Behind a film of curtains was an immense low pallet, scattered with tasseled pillows.

Talia shuddered and wrapped her arms around herself. Her body had been bathed, pampered, scented and oiled for the sheikh who was expected to arrive later. Arabic was one language she hadn't studied, but there was no denying she was in a fix. She felt like the primed and stuffed Thanksgiving turkey, properly buttered, ready for the man who was to arrive. She was certain it wasn't Kadar. He didn't act interested in her at all.

She swallowed the fear that had been nagging her since the sheikh, her previous owner, discovered her trading rock-and-roll tapes to one of his wives for the ring. The sheikh was fat, and greedy for her. He'd reluctantly sold her to a rank-pulling prince, who had arrived in full native garb, with a scimitar at his side.

In the midst of bartering, the sheikh had forgotten about the ring. Talia hadn't. She looked down, checking the ring securely tucked in the perfumed crevice of her breasts. All she had to do was steal a camel, make it across a freezing desert and slip back into her cozy stewardess outfit.

A dark-eyed woman moved swiftly toward Talia, clucking softly, comfortingly. She dabbed a silk cloth at Talia's eyes, which were lined with kohl. "Women should stick together," Talia informed her, and tried not to sniff. "I really could use good old nerdy Calum and his protective Tallchief genes now, you know."

The woman nodded as though she understood and sympathized. Talia sniffed again. "Petrovnas don't give up. Calum is the sort of sweet guy who leads a nice life in a small town—and I did like his family. Little Megan is a beautiful baby, with the Tallchiefs' gray eyes and black lashes." She shook her head at the woman, who was looking up at her sympathetically. "But, gee whiz, my auntie Em. Calum is a great kisser, but he doesn't understand Petrovna rules. He's overly protective, and exactly what I do not want after Alek, Anton and Papa. Calum can be very sexy, though. The first time he—well, you can't understand anything, so I can speak freely—I felt like I'd been claimed when he . . ."

She tried not to flush and shook her head. Calum's large hands had moved over her sweetly, possessively. His coaxing lips on her breast had drawn a taut, heated, trembling response from feminine areas she hadn't known were that sensitive. She almost wished he was here to share the sumptuous bedding with her. She'd saved herself because she valued her first experience with a man. The way Calum had looked down at her tenderly, she had known he would treasure her. She closed her eyes, hoarding the moment. Calum had fitted against her perfectly, and she had felt so safe. She could use a dose of his safety now. "It's just that I really don't want to be claimed, you know. I've been under the Petrovna males' protective thumb, and I like my life now. Lots of action and travel. Then he had to hold this baby, see? I never knew I had nerves so deep in my body, like I wanted—okay, like I wanted to have a baby...his gray-eyed, black-haired baby. Now that was frightening. I can't imagine living in one place or settling down. The whole thing is scary."

The woman smoothed Talia's long hair and murmured sympathetically as Talia continued listing her woes. "I just hope the prince didn't buy me too cheaply. That wouldn't be good for my ego." She studied the gold slave bracelet on her wrist and one on her ankle, and the tiny bells attached to them jingled merrily. "I do like the shade of red you used on my nails and toenails. Too bad you don't understand what I'm saying."

"My dear, you should be honored that the Desert Hawk, blood brother of Prince Kadar, has chosen you to warm his bed," the woman murmured as she moved gracefully away from Talia. While Talia dealt with the woman's perfect English, she paused before opening the tent's flap. "Many women have wanted him, yet he comes a long way to see his gift from Kadar."

"Wait! You *can* speak English!" Talia ran after the woman, stopped by the two burly guards at the tent's opening. She listened intently to the clamor outside the tent, shouts rising above high shrills and— Talia backed away as the guards parted and two big men stepped into the shadowy tent. She recognized Kadar instantly, but the other man stood in the shadows, his face shielded by his headgear. He motioned to Talia to come closer, and she shook her head. One of the guards gripped her arm and brought her into the light.

Kadar moved to a tray filled with liquors. He poured two small glasses and handed one to the other man in the shadows. "My brother, Hawk of the Desert, this is the woman I wish to give you. Turn around, woman, so that my brother may see you.''

Talia resisted the guard's easy turning of her body. She looked at Kadar over her shoulder, her hair whipping around her body. ''Now look here—you have no right to buy and sell women.''

The Hawk loomed over Talia, his cloaked shoulders and headdress flowing around him, blocking out everything else in the tent. His black eyes glittered, coursing slowly down her body, then back to her face. Cloth concealed his jaw, and the scent of horses and leather and man wafted around her.

She took a step back and bumped into the bodyguard. He grunted painfully and removed his foot from under hers.

''Quiet, woman. She is scrawny, Kadar. Not at all enticing,'' the man's deep voice stated arrogantly. He came closer, only his dark eyes showing between the layers of his headdress and cloak. His finger lifted and slowly traced her breasts above the ornate low bodice. He lightly prodded the soft flesh above the bodice. He peered down at her scowl as the guard held both of her upper arms. ''She is scrawny, Kadar.''

The man's big hand opened and slid slowly down Talia's side, fitting in the indentation of her waist and resting on her hip. When she eased aside, his fingers were firm. He studied her navel and the soft swell of her stomach, then possessively placed his hand over her stomach. Talia sucked in her breath, because the man's eyes were burning into her. ''Look,'' she began breathlessly as his hand circled to her back, flattened and tugged her against his unrelenting body. ''Oh—''

''My dove, why do you tremble?'' he whispered in a husky, deep voice. Then he bent to whisper in her ear, ''You want me, yes? You want to twine those long legs around me and let me drink of the wine of your body, nourish me from the strawberries upon your pale breasts and warm me with your silken hair, do you not?''

''No!'' Talia trembled at the image of the Hawk's dark body spread upon her own. She longed for good old safe Calum. She arched back, her hands outflung. ''I can pay you back. I'll go into hock. I'll borrow—''

In the shadows, Kadar laughed softly, and the Hawk's dark eyes glinted with humor. "The woman could not entice a hermit. She has nothing seductive about her. Making love with her would be like caressing a board. I find my body runs cold at the thought."

"Well. That's okay with me. Let me go." Talia watched the Hawk sweep through the tent to sprawl in the shadows beside Kadar. The two men watched her intently as musicians began to pluck small stringed instruments in a seductive beat. The wind fluttered the tent walls with a rhythm that matched the fear within Talia.

"Do not talk. Dance. Try to interest me with your scrawny body," the Hawk ordered, sipping his liquor. A woman entered with a plate of hot, spicy food and watched the Hawk with hungry eyes as she served the two lords.

Talia stood very still and tapped her toe. When the bells jingled, she stopped.

Kadar leaned toward the Hawk and grinned. "She refuses. Shall I turn her over to my men now? Or just stake her in the burning sun?"

"Perhaps she is shy. Perhaps she does not know how to please a man, or to dance as a woman."

"No and yes. I've had dance lessons." Talia inhaled, then exhaled quickly. "Look, Kadar...Hawk. If I dance for you, is that a fair trade? I mean, will you let me go?"

"Begin." The Hawk sprawled in the shadows, his dark shirt and trousers flowing along the tasseled pillows. Kadar rose in a swirl of robes as he nodded and left the tent, indicating that the musicians, the guards and the woman should follow. Outside, the musicians began again, their beat seductive.

Talia slowly moved one shoulder, a concession to the dance Hawk wanted. She tapped her toe once.

"Or we can go to bed," the Hawk murmured, a motion of his hand indicating the sprawling, pillow-laden pallet behind the silken curtains.

Talia rotated her other shoulder, a bit more quickly. She bit her lip. She swallowed and began to sway with the music, intending to dance as long as the Hawk stayed awake. Then she'd borrow that huge-looking dagger he'd placed on his discarded cloak, slit a hole in the tent and escape. She moved toward him in the lamplight and refilled his glass to the brim. "You must be very thirsty after a hard day at riding the desert."

"I prefer your body without clothing." The Hawk's hand flicked open one tiny pearl button on her bodice. Then he reached for the glass and drained it slowly, while keeping her startled stare locked with his. "What is this?" The tip of his little finger caught in Una's ring and tugged.

"That is the reason I came here. I need the ring to—"

She didn't trust the way his expression immediately tensed, the way his eyes pinned hers. Talia leaped to her feet, clutching the tiny bodice to her. This man frightened her.

She saw none of Calum's tenderness in the hot-eyed Hawk. She held her bodice and poured another glass of potent liquor for him. With any luck, he'd pass out and she could make her escape. All she had to do was dance and keep his glass filled, and then she'd make her way back to Calum. She wanted him to hold her and comfort her. She would take his ring back to him and finish off Olson and find a way to make Calum her first lover. She'd soothe the shadows within him. He could do with a little chaos in his life. And a little tenderness. She would find her way back to him, grab the Tallchief stone and seize Calum Tallchief.

"Drink up. I feel like dancing."

Six

When at last Talia slept on the carpet, Calum lifted her in his arms and carried her to his bed. She hadn't noticed that his glass had been regularly emptied into a vase. Her sensuous dance, a subtle mixture of eye-popping quivers, had strained his body until he wondered if he'd recover. Her dance had been a war of wills, and for once Calum couldn't rely on his control. Finally, clearly exhausted, she had danced slower and slower until she had wilted magnificently upon the lush, huge flowers of the carpet. Una's garnet ring gleamed bloodred on Talia's finger, and Calum raised it to his lips. He had placed the ring upon her finger, and he would keep her safe.

Talia purred softly in her sleep and pressed against him as he wrapped them together in the thick silken quilt. Calum eased the string of pearls away from her forehead and gathered her closer. Talia, in a seductive mode, was a sight Calum didn't want another man to experience.

He slid the tinted black lenses from his eyes and placed them in a container. Black eyes went well with the deeper tan he had acquired under Fiona's old sunlamp.

"Mmm...Calum..." she murmured drowsily against his throat, and eased a long leg over his, her arms encircling his neck.

He held very still, his body aroused against her softness. He realized suddenly and to his horror that droplets of sweat had appeared on his forehead. Even sleeping, the woman was a disaster, a willful, thankless—

She moved over him, her hips undulating slightly against him as she whispered drowsily, "Darn. I ache all over. I know you're just a dream, but I'd really like to—"

Calum nuzzled her ear. The concession reached inside him; he realized how tenderly he felt toward her. She'd come home to rest, like a tired kitten, and he wanted to cuddle her.

"Calum, do you suppose you could..." He thought she was sleeping, but then she moved restlessly, placing his hand upon her breast. "Mmm... Like that." Then she slid off into sleep, leaving him cupping her breast and his body aching.

Talia hugged the silken quilt up to her chin. This was her second night in the tent, and desert nights were cold. Though he was gone, Hawk's presence filled their bed. He'd been off doing desert things during the day, and the entire tent had been stripped of anything she could use for clothing to escape. Again, she had been bathed, kneaded, buttered in scents and oils and left to await Hawk's arrival. Because she was aching from hours of dancing for Hawk, Talia had asked for several baths and massages during the day. It had become clear after her first tentative tries for clothing that the entire encampment was loyal to Prince Kadar's blood brother, the Desert Hawk.

Talia held up Una's ring, the three bloodred garnets set in a golden Celtic design. At least she had the Tallchief ring. The gold slave bracelets, with their bells, jingled on her wrist and on her ankle. She sniffed and dabbed the quilt to her eyes, drying them as the wind billowed inside the tent. Wind billowing in the tent was the signal that someone had arrived; it was more effective than a doorbell.

She heard Hawk speak quietly to the serving girl who had brought him dinner.

The tent quieted, and the lamps were extinguished. Talia's heart raced until the Desert Hawk swept into her veiled bedroom. He wore his robes. "So my bride anxiously awaits me," he murmured in a deep, satisfied drawl.

"Bride?" Talia went very still and blinked. "I missed that part."

He lifted a brow, his eyes black and smoldering in the dim light as they swept slowly, possessively, over her. Talia pulled the quilt up to her shoulders, only to have it slowly pulled downward by a stronger hand. He stared at her body, which instantly flushed. "So shy? I thought we dispensed with that last night."

Talia pressed her thighs together and ran a thorough quick inventory of her intimate parts as Hawk knelt down on the bed.

"Run that bride part by me again?" she asked, edging away from him.

"Surely, after last night, you have no doubts as to my claim. How you danced with ecstasy for me. Come here, my desert lily, let us begin...."

Hawk eased beneath the quilt, and Talia scooted to the other side of the bed. Talia stared at him. "Now, just a minute—"

Talia shivered, then flushed. She was finding it hard to breathe, and she stood, holding a fringed pillow to her as a shield. "Don't you have a camel to wash?"

The Hawk's dark eyes glinted in the shadows as he studied her. "Come...no need to be shy, after last night. You want me. Say it. Say it, or I will make you say it."

For the first time in her life, Talia Petrovna was scared. "Uh...I...I can't. I've got this sweet guy at home. Calum Tallchief. He's rather sweet—"

"You have no other man but me," the Hawk stated, in a low, primitive tone resembling a panther's growl. "But you amuse me. Tell me about this man."

"He loves computers. I think he's buried himself in them because he's mourning his wife. She was killed in an accident just months after they married," she managed.

He frowned thoughtfully. "Surely he would not like computers more than a woman as fiery as you. Tell me more."

"He likes order, which drives me nuts. His clothes are all organized in his closet . . . dull gray suits—" She sucked in her breath as Hawk rose from the bed and stood staring at her.

"You are shy. Yet you want me."

"I want only one man." Her voice surprised her; it was strong and firm.

His black eyes probed hers. "You love this Calum?"

"He's sweet. Safe and controlling. He reminds me of my brothers and my father. Very old-fashioned."

Talia cried out as Hawk slowly walked to her, lifted her and carried her to the bed.

He tossed her upon the pillows, and when she began to scramble away, he caught her ankle and gently dragged her back, following her down into the sumptuous bedding. He caught both her flying wrists in one hand, held them above her head. "My dove, you will tell me of this Calum. Now."

She wiggled beneath him, then as his gaze shot down her pale body, she stilled. "I told you. Calum is sweet and old-fashioned."

"Sweet?" Hawk bent to taste her inner wrist, lightly running his tongue across it. His big hand eased down to possessively claim her hips and raise her to him. "Like this?"

"He's more . . . mental. He's very controlled. He wears a pocket protector."

"Ah, I see. A boring nerd. Yet you cry out beneath him? You want the heat of his body in you, filling you to the hilt, taking you to ecstacy—"

She looked away and flushed as he stared down at her body, pale against his, his eyes glittering beneath his lashes. "We're very . . . very hot for each other," she managed valiantly, and tossed back a phrase as eloquent as his. "My skin tingles with each touch. His eyes are the color of the mountain storms, or as clear and hard as steel. He's delicious, like a nice, tasty . . . pomegranate or a cherry sundae with whipped cream."

She changed the fruit-and-ice-cream image to one more masculine. "Like a big black stallion. With stormy eyes. Mmm . . . hot. That is how I feel with him. All that, and he manages to be rather . . . innocent and sweet, too."

Hawk lifted a black eyebrow. "Hot? You want him? Even though I want you? Even though the bud of your desire awaits my touch? Even though the promise of your body comes from the perfume of your skin, the honeyed liquid of—"

"That is very descriptive language," Talia managed shakily.

"My hot-blooded temptress, I fear I am too tired to amuse you. Perhaps tomorrow night," he murmured after a yawn. Then he eased away and turned his back to her.

Trembling, Talia stared at him. *Who was he to be scheduling lovemaking she didn't want?*

"Come." Hawk reached behind him to draw her arm around him. He sighed and nestled his hard-muscled back against the pillows. "We sleep. Perhaps, if you are good, I will take you in the night— Ouch!" He rubbed the hair on his chest that had just been pulled, and then he chuckled, flattening her hand on his muscled stomach. "Oh, no, my pigeon. Your impatience for me must wait."

"We can't sleep all night like this," she began, and found that he held her gently when she tried to move away.

"Mmm, *chérie.* Can we not?" Hawk snuggled deeper in her clasp and breathed deeply.

Talia decided not to test her good luck. When Hawk slept deeply, she'd grab the nearest camel and—Talia yawned and closed her eyes; she'd rest until then.

In the night, she dreamed Calum was kissing her thoroughly, and she reveled in the slow, dreamy sensuality of being well loved from head to toe. Of being touched intimately, and rising to the delicious torment of his hands and mouth, to the loving that took her higher until she burst. Then the gentle whispers of Hawk awoke her—

The Desert Hawk! Her eyes popped open to full morning, and she lay very still, running through an inventory of her body. She knew instinctively that he hadn't touched her. Talia was waiting for him when he entered the veiled bedroom. He didn't stand a chance. "Real clothes would be nice. Just any old thing you could spare." She shivered and drew the quilt higher. "You've got to let me go."

His arrogance flicked at her. "I cannot. You are mine. You wear my ring."

"It's my ring. I traded it for Huey Lewis tapes. I'm going to trade it to Calum for—"

"Admit you do not care for this Calum."

"He's a great guy. I may even love him. I may want to bear his child. The Tallchiefs have beautiful gray-eyed children—" Talia's defiance was rewarded by Hawk flipping her onto her back.

He lay over her, arrogant, strong, and easily stilling her. "You *may* love him?"

"I have a . . . certain tenderness for him. I've been saving myself for a sweet guy like him."

He bent to nuzzle her throat. "Have you?"

Hawk began to grin, and then to chuckle. He reached to light the lamp.

Slowly Hawk removed his robes and tinted lenses, and Talia found herself staring up into the hard, determined face and gray eyes of Calum Tallchief.

"You!" Talia yelled indignantly, and flung herself at him.

An hour later, Calum sat behind Talia on his horse. Wrapped in his cloak against the chill, she sat very straight, with a heavy guilt around her. She hadn't spoken to him since that first "You!" She refused to be logical, to discuss the lesson he hoped he had taught her.

Calum began to feel very uneasy; the ramrod set of her shoulders was not forgiving. Talia was an emotional woman; perhaps he had gone too far. "It was for your own good, Talia. To teach you a lesson. One wrong move and you'll stay here with Kadar until I deal with Olson."

Unused to dealing with a woman he wanted desperately, Calum resented his lack of past experience.

Talia eyed him over her shoulder, then turned away, her shoulders rigid. Calum inhaled grimly, guiding the horse easily toward the waiting airplane. He glanced at the ring on Talia's finger, the bloodred garnets catching the morning sun, and wondered why this one woman could drive him to distraction. He preferred her temper and Petrovna curses to her silence.

That night at Calum's house, Talia noisily barricaded her room while Calum called Alek. Her brother roared with laughter. When Calum carefully added they had shared a bed, Alek swore passionately and demanded to know Calum's intentions. "Keep her," Calum responded, listening to more furniture thumping against the walls. "We're not to the logical discussion point yet."

"Logic?" Alek began to laugh again. "Whose? Yours or hers?"

Talia burst into Calum's office, her hands on her hips, her legs wide in their knee-high black-heeled boots. Her breasts shimmered palely above the black leather bustier. "Did we or did we not have sex?" she demanded.

"Sex?" There was a brief pause on Alek's end of the telephone line before he started yelling in an outraged tone. He muttered something between curses, and another dark, menacing male voice began yelling. A woman began wailing about her sweet little girl without a white wedding dress. She used the word *beast,* frequently, and Calum realized that he was probably the beast in question.

"Talia is all right, and in mint condition," Calum managed steadily before hanging up the phone. He caught the statue Talia had just flung at him.

"You mean—? You mean to tell me that I wasn't seductive enough—? That you really weren't interested—? What am I, boring? How dare you!" she stated indignantly as the phone began ringing. She jerked it from its cradle and snapped, "Alek. Papa. This one is mine." Then she slapped the receiver into the cradle. "You low-down—"

He tried logic. "Talia. When I make love to a woman, she knows it."

She tilted her head, her eyes darkening dangerously. Her voice had a deadly, controlled purr. She was wearing black, her black boots braced wide apart, her hands on her hips. She looked glorious, powerful...enchanting. Talia whipped back a gleaming pale strand of hair. "You mean that, as a man, you pick the time and the place?"

"Rules, Talia. Men usually—" Calum ran his hand through his hair. It had been a long, hard, silent day, and Calum ached to have a calm discussion with her, to reason with her about the danger in which she had placed herself and to explain that someone had to take care of her. He would wait until Talia's mood burned itself out, and then they'd have a nice calm discussion—

"Whose rules?" she demanded, grabbing a fistful of his shirt. He winced as she pulled the hair on his chest with it. He hated wincing, Calum decided darkly. Only Talia could extract that expression from him.

"My rules." Then he reached for her, tugged her into his arms and kissed her hungrily.

What began as frustration became a softness flowing between them. Talia's lips lifted for his, shifting, brushing, heating.... Calum held very still as she eased closer to him. He didn't trust her, not a bit— He carefully placed his hands on her waist, because they badly wanted to wander to softer places.

To his surprise, she melted against him and snuggled her face into his throat. "Calum, why did you come after me?"

He lowered his lashes to study her. There he was, all ready to be logical and explain the danger.... But the vulnerable tremble in her voice could be faked.... She could be gathering ammunition to— Calum flung all caution to the winds, and realized to his horror that he was absolutely involved with the life and adventures of Talia Petrovna. He nuzzled her cheek, and sensed a homecoming when she held very still. He cautiously pressed closer and sensed a warmth that he had missed his entire adult life. He kissed her temple, then her cheek, then eased her head upon his shoulder. She was his to take care of, his life's mate. He rubbed the back of her head, experimenting with the places that might soothe her. She began to purr softly, the response encouraging him.

Talia looked up at him, and he smiled tenderly at her. He went light-headed with relief.

That was what he wanted with Talia. A life of holding her, of children— He wanted to claim her, to make her his, to care for her, to protect her and hold her in his arms. He found her pouting lower lip and bit it gently. Talia sighed and placed her hands on his cheeks. "Tell me, Calum. Tell me why you brought me here. Why you came after me, and why you brought me back here. Tell me."

She held very still as he kissed her cheeks, her lashes, her nose, and brushed her chin. "Calum. Words. Say them. I need to know."

Calum wrapped her in his arms and stood very still. He'd never shared his heart with anyone, and he wasn't certain he could. Talia nestled closer and sighed. "This is good. But, Calum, you know I can't let you get away with this. Not without a good reason."

The question slid across his lips, a raw invitation that he knew she'd refuse. "Will you stay here with me?"

"Calum, you must have loved her so much." The illogical sequence of her statement caught him broadside. Leave it to Talia to shift from the required yes or no. Their conversation was on a different plane now, a very iffy plane, and a wrong answer could send her running.

Calum realized that he had to express himself to her, a difficult task for a man who shared nothing of himself. He realized with a sinking feeling that Talia was giving him the opportunity to tell her how he felt. A cold fist slammed into his stomach as he realized that he might fail this important test. He'd always found his privacy safer, but now he risked losing Talia— He moved away from her, and ran his hands through his hair. He stood to look out at the mountains, his hands tucked into his back pockets. "Sherry demanded, and got, male attention. She was beautiful and we—were passionately involved. We were either fighting or loving. I wanted more. Logically, we had to have some middle ground for the marriage to survive. Some common interests—"

Talia moved against his back, taking his hands from his pockets and wrapping her hands around his waist. She leaned against him, nuzzling his back. "I was jealous," Calum continued, lacing his fingers with hers. "She liked that . . . called it 'our common interest.' I thought I could handle the situation, turn it into what my parents had, something solid. We were on our way up, young, hungry, savvy executives. Our marriage should have worked. But our fights got more intense, and after one, Sherry got into her car and ran into a truck."

Talia rocked him gently and kissed the back of his neck. "You can't control love, Calum. Or people."

"Love? We had nothing like that. It ended that night. Maybe I could have stopped her, I don't know. I'll never know if we could have strengthened our marriage and made it last."

"You were shattered. You think it was your fault."

He hated admitting his vulnerability. "Maybe. I just know it ended wrong."

"It wasn't a clean wrap, with all the ends neatly tucked in place." Talia moved around to slide into his arms. She looked up at him, smoothing his cheeks. Calum gave himself over to her fingertips, letting them soothe the slicing pain within him.

"Calum, I'll stay here, and you go out into the world and do your warrior deeds. Joust with Olson. I suspect that you're just like all the Tallchief males, despite your modern-man exterior. But I'm not going to make it easy for you. I've never done this before, and I'm definitely not going to release you until I've had my full revenge. My brothers and Papa won't be happy with you if I stay. You can certainly count on them arriving in full temper, demanding that you marry me."

Her gaze slid away from his. "I . . . You have no idea how embarrassing they can be. Please don't take their threats seriously. I have no intention of getting married. I get this terrible choked feeling just thinking about it."

"Will you stay?" Calum fought the fear within him. He didn't want to lose her, and it wasn't like Talia to concede easily. He could be making a mistake by leaving her—

"Yes. You can trust me to stay. But I don't promise to make it easy on you, you rat. I can't deal with secrets, and you're loaded with them. I suspect you inherited your stoic silence from your great-great-grandfather. I'm not the settling-down kind, and I'm still very miffed at your interference in my capers. That Desert Hawk escapade still deserves payback. I count on you for logic. You scare me, Calum. You're a man who wants everything, and—'' she frowned up at him ''—I'm not certain I can fit into your life, even for a short time. Any man who would make a woman wonder if she hadn't just dreamed they'd . . . they'd made love . . .''

Calum lifted a mocking eyebrow. ''How do you know we haven't?''

She didn't trust his teasing expression. ''I think I would remember. From now on, don't play games. You're too effective when you do, and I don't trust you.''

''Rules? From Talia Petrovna?''

''I'm making new ones for you.'' She frowned up at him. ''Oh, Calum, I'm so scared. This isn't what I want. *You* aren't what I want. I've never wanted an affair with a man like you . . . possessive, dominating, macho, scheming, devious—''

''Affair?'' The word slammed into Calum, but he decided not to confront Talia until he had considered his options. An affair with her wasn't the long-term commitment he wanted. ''After you're safe from Olson's reach, we'll discuss everything logically. Together.'' He understood. She wasn't used to letting anyone share her life. Neither was he.

She shook her head, and a sleek swath of hair swirled around his wrist, soothing him. ''Logically? Calum, you never change.''

''I will try. Just don't leave me.'' Very gently, Calum enfolded her in his arms. She held him fiercely, and for now, it was enough.

After he kissed her at her bedroom door, Calum stopped in the hallway and looked back at her. He didn't trust her expression. Talia had plans, and leaving her now could mean disaster. Taking her with him would definitely be a disaster and put her in danger. He found himself anticipating what her next move would be, and he walked back to her. He removed the stone from his neck. ''Will you wear this?''

She accepted his placing of the stone upon her, a ceremony that he discovered was very important to him. She accepted his light kiss and moved slowly backward into her room, closing the door firmly against him.

Calum stared at the door. Talia definitely had plans of her own, and they included a measure of revenge against him. Calum found himself smiling.

In the morning, Talia walked Calum to his car. She'd decided to teach Calum a lesson—to take revenge upon him for his interruption of her capers and for using logic when he should have used romance. Talia allowed herself a small smile. Her disguise this morning was the first of many. Calum would learn not to interfere with her life. He would soon learn that living with her was not an easy road.

Because Calum was a delicate man, Talia realized that his male ego demanded that he take care of the Olson situation. She also realized from life with her family that the male ego was a fragile flower and honor had to be served.

His arm had been around her, his hand resting on her hip. He hadn't said anything about her hair up in curlers, her cut-off sweatpants and T-shirt or his old flannel bathrobe. He didn't seem to notice her mud mask, though she didn't trust the humorous glint in his sea-gray eyes. She'd promised to stay, but she hadn't promised to make it easy for him. She wanted to let him know that she wasn't always glamorous or sweet. But she also wanted him to know that she wasn't a wilting Nellie when times got tough.

She handed him his briefcase and sighed. "You'd better do a good job on Olson. Are you certain that you don't need me? I mean, I can be ready in no time. I'll go like this— I can change in the car."

"That's an interesting offer. But I want you safely away from Olson. From the messages on my recorder, he's out for blood. But no more than Alek or your father. After all, what's one more enraged male? No, you stay here, out of temptation's path. You were right about them asking my intentions. Your father demanded that you have extra locks on your door, with one key—yours."

She looked away as he paused, studying her intently. She would have to lay down the rules for her family, to protect

Calum. She wouldn't have him forced into marriage, or into a commitment to her.

She eyed the man she'd once thought of as a nerd. All the danger of the Hawk was there, just below the surface. She smoothed his suit-clad shoulder and straightened his lapel. Calum's eyes flickered with suspicion; his large hand locked firmly on her hip. "What are you up to, Talia?"

"Me?" She fluttered her lashes. Calum smelled delicious, all freshly showered and shaved. She touched his gleaming black lashes. Not every cowboy could play a sheikh like Calum. "Trusting someone else to pull a caper isn't that easy," she admitted reluctantly. "You don't know what you're asking of me. I'm not a damsel in distress. I can take care of myself. I'm a hands-on person."

"You stay out of trouble." He kissed her nose, his hand caressing her waist. "I'll take care of the hands-on."

His sensual challenge made her catch her breath. She studied his expressions. It was all there, the tender desire, the need, the danger, and the shadows of his past.... She ached for Calum's dark side, the pain kept tightly inside him. And the loneliness that he had not shared with anyone. "I'm not promising anything, and I want to know every detail. Calum, it is important that you do not use physical violence on Olson. I detest violence. I don't expect you to lower yourself to physical vengeance—it's so crude. That is exactly the reason I did not want Alek, Anton or Papa involved. I have confidence in your logic, without brute force."

"So you trust me?" The question was laden with meanings she didn't want to consider.

"I have a certain faith that when you promise to do a job, you do your best," she returned. He chuckled, and she loved the deep, rich sound. She, Talia Petrovna, was now playing the waiting housekeeper, while her knight leaped into his black four-wheeler and rushed off to save the kingdom.

She *did* trust him. Good old logical Calum. She lifted aside his suit jacket to find his pocket protector, neatly lined with pens. The sight was reassuring. Talia realized that she wanted him wearing his official gear when he was within reach of other women.

She realized with horror that she was slightly jealous and very possessive.

Calum was going to where women would find him enchanting and probably try to— "Wear your pocket protector.... Uh...protection for your shirts."

He frowned curiously, and she wondered about protection. Specifically about Calum and protection and herself.

About gray-eyed Tallchief babies and Calum.

About sharing his life. About giving and taking and sharing. She realized there was one area in which she would not share Calum Tallchief—that was with another woman. He looked too luscious to release into the wild, too tempting to expose to other women. She blinked. Except for his darkened gray eyes upon her and his alert expression, he was the same old Calum, corporate troubleshooter.

Talia inhaled the fresh, crisp late-October air and went dizzy. She, Talia Petrovna, who had always waltzed away from deepening relationships, wanted to cuddle Calum. Not every cowboy would appreciate a goodbye kiss from a woman with a mud mask on her face and curlers in her hair. It had taken her an eternity and ten empty frozen orange juice containers to create the proper curler look.

She wondered if Calum knew she had crept into his bed last night and cuddled up to his broad, warm, safe back. She grinned up at him as he studied her curlers as though he were placing her in a picture frame. His intent stare caused her to be nervous. "Like it? The little-housekeeper outfit?"

"I get the idea that you're out for revenge, and this outfit is just the start. By the way, your distributor cap is back on."

Talia grinned. "My, my... Do *you* trust *me?*"

"In some things, yes." Calum moved to shield her from curious eyes. He ran his fingertip slowly down her throat to her breasts and then across them. His hand flattened gently, finding the stone beneath her clothing. "You're up to something, and I've got the feeling that I'm going to pay for collecting you. Whatever you decide to do about me, just stay here. I want you safe. My family will take care of you," he whispered slowly, meaningfully.

She realized that now he was vulnerable, asking instead of ordering her.

She frowned slightly, feeling childish at being bothered by his admission of desire for his wife. Talia was inexperienced, and— He moved her hips against his taut body. "You do that to me, Petrovna. Every time I look at you. Last night, very little kept me from coming to you. I'm glad you came to me."

She flushed, uncertain of her need of him. "You should have told me you were awake. I couldn't sleep and needed something to cuddle. You're warm and hairy, like my favorite old teddy bear."

He laughed outright and drew her hand lower to cover him. "And not exactly soft." He placed her hands upon his cheeks, turning them to kiss her palms, one by one. Over their joined hands, his eyes were dark and making promises that frightened and excited her.

Calum's warm gaze slid from her to over her head. His smile died as he watched Birk approach them on his motorcycle. Talia watched, fascinated, as Calum's features hardened and his arm reached out to draw her close in a possessive gesture. She thought the gesture was sweet. His kiss wasn't. It left her dizzy and hungry. Then he nodded curtly and slid into his vehicle and drove off.

"Wait!" Talia motioned to Birk, then hopped on the back of his motorcycle, and they sped off after Calum. He pulled over to the side of the road with a wary, resigned expression on his face. "What is the Tallchief legend that goes with the ring, Calum?"

Birk turned his back, clearly giving them privacy. Calum stared at the road, at Birk, then lashed a glance at her. He distinctly looked cornered, as though he were looking for an escape. "I suppose you'll threaten me with dire consequences if I don't tell you." His sigh was heavy with resignation. "Come here."

Birk began chuckling, and Calum scowled at him. He glared at her, his expression that of a brooding, resentful male. "Now isn't the time, Talia."

"Now, Tallchief." She wasn't budging an inch.

His scowl deepened, and his tone was neither sweet nor romantic as he explained the legend. "When a man of Fearghus blood places the ring upon the right woman's finger, he'll capture his true love forever. There, that's it. Are you satisfied?"

Stunned by the romantic legend, Talia looked down at the ring on her finger and then at Calum. "It's just a legend. Don't get terrified," he muttered darkly. "Be here when I get back."

"Oh, fine. The ring is supposed to be special, and you've wasted it on me." Tears burned Talia's lids. Here was a perfectly wonderful romantic legend, and Calum had no idea of the value— Calum closed his eyes and shook his head. She'd wait for him—something she'd done for no one else. She'd be trustworthy—and perhaps even prepare him for the woman who *should* wear the ring.

Meanwhile, it fitted her perfectly and looked wonderful against her skin. Just as Calum did. He was actually a nice big snuggly teddy bear, of a species temporarily endangered by Alek, Anton and Papa Petrovna. She'd have to keep him safe for his "true love." "Goodbye, Calum, darlin'," she whispered meekly.

He scowled, clearly not trusting her tone. His expression ran through a series of dissecting, curious and suspicious looks that Talia returned with a blithe smile. "Go on, now. Shoo. Ride off and fight the world. Joust. Throw spears. Call if you need backup...."

She watched his vehicle drive away, aware of his uncertain study in the rearview mirror. She waved happily to him. "Poor Calum. He really needs me, Birk. Doesn't he? As a housekeeper," she added cautiously.

"Ah, yes. I purely believe he does. His life has been too easy up until he met you." Then Birk began grinning. "You intend to teach him a lesson, don't you?"

She grinned back. "Come back to the house for breakfast. I've got lots of orange juice. I'll tell you about Calum when he was the Desert Hawk. I knew all along who he was and that he was out to give me some sort of obscure lesson. He's such a romantic."

Talia ignored Birk's disbelieving snort to glance down at the gleaming garnets. She liked wearing Calum's ring to remind her of him. She tightened her hand into a fist, keeping his ring safe.

Seven

That afternoon, Lacey's parachute drifted closer to Talia's. "What do you mean, it's nice for a time? The Tallchiefs aren't the kind of people who drift in and out of lives, Talia. They've been taking care of me since I can remember. Calum isn't the kind of man to take a relationship lightly. He took his wife's death very badly. He was totally dedicated to preserving their relationship, and she put him through hell."

Talia concentrated on the cow field below them, their target landing site. "He's delicate in some ways. I'm afraid I'll hurt him. He's got this thing about ends being tied up neatly. I don't know that my life is neat, or that I can change. I've always detested order and systems, and Calum wants everything. I'm just not a built-to-stay person, Lacey."

Talia glanced down at Duncan and Birk, on the ground, their hands on their hips as they looked up. "Look down there. Look at those frowns. Calum is just like them, afraid for me. I've lived a life of doing as I please. I'm past the idealistic stage of my girlhood. At my age, a good percentage of women have been married and divorced and are struggling to survive."

"You're afraid." Lacey's blue eyes were serious, framed by her helmet and her windswept mop of black curls.

"Basically. And I resent promising Calum that I would stay here. He's like that, expecting things from me."

"What do you expect from him?"

"I'd like him to be happy. That's why I agreed to stay, because it seemed to comfort him. And to teach him a lesson for his own good."

Lacey laughed out loud. "Yeah. Right. No selfish reasons tucked in there at all, right?"

They sailed on the wind, lowering slowly into the pasture. "I do not like domineering men. My family is filled with them. Calum shows the same tendencies. Eventually—" As they expertly landed in the field, Talia looked at Duncan and Birk. They stood, long-legged Westerners framed by a backdrop of snowcapped mountains. The grim set of their jaws, and their arms, folded disapprovingly over their chests, reminded her of Calum.

A long-term relationship with Calum wouldn't be good for either one of them. Rules weren't for her—except Petrovna's Law.

She touched the Tallchief stone beneath her scarlet jumpsuit; the garnets on her finger caught the brilliant afternoon sunlight. She wore the mark of his possession, light tethers to a relationship she hadn't wanted.

Calum didn't need more pain; he'd had enough. So had she.

Talia inhaled with resignation. "My family won't understand if I stay. They'll consider it my first commitment. You don't know them. I've been running from that long white dress for years. I don't want Calum forced into anything illogical."

Lacey laughed again; it was a musical sound. "Duncan didn't want an affair with Sybil. I doubt that Calum would stand for anything less than a wedding ring."

"He can be just awful. Arrogant and rude. He gets this warrior attitude about me, and I rise to the bait every time. He's old-fashioned and outdated and it sets me off. I'm still furious with him over that Desert Hawk incident. I lost a measure of confidence on that caper. I'm usually quite successful. He was totally arrogant, and payback is definitely needed.''

"You're afraid, and none of what you're saying really is enough reason to walk away from something good.''

Talia closed her eyes and let the old pain swirl around her. "I can't go through it again. I almost got married once, and he walked at the last minute.'' The memory slammed deep within Talia, who realized her pride had not yet been salved. She vividly remembered the people sitting in the church, saw their sympathetic expressions as she escaped her shame, dressed in her wedding dress. Talia hated the tears that began flowing easily, chilling her cheeks.

Lacey gave Talia a quick hug. "Calum keeps his promises. The Tallchiefs always do.'' Lacey spoke quietly and from years of experience. She bent to scoop up her parachute from the ground. "Take a note. The Tallchiefs are bred to hold what is theirs. Calum has never looked at a woman like he looks at you.''

"The whole thing is scary.''

"Think of it as jumping out of a plane. Or surfing the best wave yet. Or climbing a mountain. Maybe a relationship is something you have to work at. Like an acquired skill.''

Talia scooped up her parachute. Calum was years ahead of her in certain skills, like lovemaking. She intended to catch up and make it an equal game; she was a woman of action, and not one to wait. She studied the sheer wall of rock on Tallchief Mountain and knew it was a challenge she had to take. "I'm dying to scale that— So what about Birk and your relationship? It's definitely not a smooth one.''

Lacey looked at her with surprise. "You're kidding. The only relationship Birk and I have is the Tallchief family. I'm almost one of them, and that's why I have the right to bring his arrogant nose down a notch. And I wouldn't try scaling that rock wall without help.''

The two weeks away from Talia were the longest of Calum's life. In the second week of November, he drove urgently toward Amen Flats, aware, to his distaste, that he was breaking the speed laws—something he had never done. He didn't trust

Talia to be where he had last put her. His four-wheeler soared through the moonlight as Calum grimly concentrated on the very neat wrap-up job he'd done, extracting Talia and the Petrovnas from suspicion.

Volatile in-laws-to-be like the Petrovnas had to be protected.

Calum gripped the steering wheel tightly and swerved around a lonely curve, the tires squalling and spraying fallen leaves.

In one week and one month, she'd turned the order in his life upside down. He had tossed away caution and decided to marry Talia Petrovna. That would eliminate interference from the protective Petrovna males. Marriage would keep her near, touchable, and under control. All he had to do now was make himself appealing as a life mate to Talia. He would approach her with logic . . . once he found her.

She was frightened of the commitment he badly wanted. Calum cursed the man who had deserted an eighteen-year-old girl at the altar.

Alek hadn't meant to let that tidbit slip, but to Calum, Talia's past experience explained everything logically.

Calum pushed away his fears that he might not appeal to Talia. He did not want to be compared to her passionate, yelling, protective male family members. He wanted her to see him as . . . valuable. A commodity she wanted very much.

Not that he could trust Talia. The morning he left, she'd tucked him in his car too easily. He'd had two long, tense weeks of waiting for her to pounce on Olson. After the first week of nightly telephone calls to her, Calum's body had ached. He did not doubt that Talia had deliberately underlined her husky, unspoken invitation to him on the telephone. He glanced at the reflective eyes of deer at the side of the road, and barely missed a skunk. He braked carefully, so as not to alarm the animal. His hands, encased in black leather gloves, ached from gripping the steering wheel, from the tense fear consuming him.

Cleaning up after Talia had required a second week—Talia's ingenious sabotage of Unique's systems had taken time to unravel. Calum allowed himself a tight, proud smile. He impatiently loosened his designer tie. Talia showed an aptitude for computers, and was capable of wrecking any system.

Including his personal safety-protection system. Sherry had been very capable. Calum scowled at the silvery disk in the sky and knew that only one woman could make him howl at the moon. Talia had been very effective. He wanted her on another level than sex—though at the moment, a good dose of it would have calmed the tension humming through him. Visions of her shimmering in red and gold and dancing for him in the desert haunted him.

Calum grimly forced away that body-jolting image and concentrated on driving. She hadn't answered his calls the second week, and Olson had felt the brunt of Calum's taut nerves. He almost regretted rapping Olson's knuckles with a file dedicated to sexual harassment statements from former employees. Jan and Roy's marriage was one among many that had suffered. Added to Olson's blatant misuse of company resources, Calum had plenty of ammunition to force the sleazeball into a tight corner. Olson had gladly set up a trust to anonymously pay cash to those he had injured. Then he'd made the mistake of pushing Calum, who dissected his past errors with the neat, effective skill of a surgeon.

At the time, Calum had controlled his need to brawl, to vent his frustration about Talia. In the end, Olson had whimpered for his job, which disgusted Calum. He really needed just one shot at Olson, a physical one, but the man's cowering had stopped him. That end would have to remain untied. He'd countered with an anonymous file, sent to Olson's wife. As a woman scorned, she would know how to use the information effectively.

Calum turned his mind to Talia. If she knew how badly he wanted her, how he lay awake wanting her in his arms, she'd be frightened. Hell, he frightened himself. Lovemaking with Talia approached an obsession that he wouldn't let out of control. She deserved tenderness, and the knowledge that he was committed.

Okay. He was committed to getting Talia into bed. But he wanted their relationship to have everything she deserved. He wanted a strong foundation. He would learn how to relate his emotions.

All right, so he didn't know if he could give her everything she needed. He didn't know about loving a woman the way Talia deserved, a sweet, old-fashioned love like his parents'. After Sherry, he doubted that he was capable. But he'd give Talia everything he could, starting with marriage. Was it enough?

Calum reluctantly admitted he hadn't given everything to his wife. He'd had sex with her, nothing more.

With Talia, his emotions caught him, tossed him in a jasmine-scented wind with passion and with tenderness. She excited the primitive hunter in him, stirred the lover who touched her with trembling hands, as if opening a delicate flower especially made for him.

He had to give her time to adjust, yet his instincts told him to claim her.

The tires squalled as he rounded a corner. Calum realized that he had never really tried to seduce or invite a woman into his firmly closed inner sanctum. There was no reason to expect Talia to act like other women—she'd just stepped into his life.

A cold mountain mist enveloped him. *Was she gone?* Her frumpy-little-housewife disguise zipped through his mind again. He studied the car ahead of him, and the woman snuggled close to the driver. That was what Calum wanted, Talia snuggled close to him.

His lower body coiled into a hot, heavy knot as he remembered her beneath his touch . . . the soft, fragrant petals of her body—

Calum gripped the steering wheel with aching hands and shifted restlessly in his seat. Hell. He wasn't a kid anymore. He knew all the dirty facts of life, and he hated loose ends. He'd kept his life neat. Then Talia had bewitched him. Moved right into the aching abyss he called his heart and started dreams of home and babies and warm, cuddly nights when they were ninety. He couldn't remember excitement before Talia. Calum pushed down on the accelerator, passing the lovers' car.

He was an idiot to think that her role as his housekeeper was believable. He felt like a sitting duck, waiting for disaster, which would arrive at Talia's choosing. One of his rules had always been self-protection, never leaving himself open to disaster. With Talia, he had little choice.

He sped toward an empty house. He couldn't remember ever wanting to return home so desperately as he did now. And Talia was gone. No doubt he'd catch her scent, and that would have to be enough. He'd rest for the night, lick his lonely wounds and then track her. Wearily Calum stopped the car and studied the darkened house. He'd find her, and hold a very tight rein on the passion that engulfed him every time he looked at her. His need for her went much deeper than love-making, he admitted tiredly, extracting himself from his rig. The angles of his contemporary home loomed cold and sterile in the moonlight, like his life without Talia.

She was gone. He was certain of it. The fire and gold she'd brought into his life was gone. The thought lodged in Calum's mind like a cold, hard brick. He felt drained and old.

For once he dismissed his laptop computer, leaving it in the car. He braced himself against the house and began to walk up the walkway to his porch.

A low, feral growl stopped him. An experienced hunter, Calum realized that the dog was big and mean and ready to protect his territory. "Easy, boy."

The massive dog moved slowly, his growl deep and menacing. He planted his four paws firmly apart, ready to defend his home. The huge hot-pink bow artfully tied around his neck was at odds with his bared fangs. Calum braced himself against the beast's assault and moved slowly toward the house. He was tired, lacking sleep, and not in the mood to wrestle with the fanged monster. The beast prepared to spring, and Calum leaped to a nearby tree. After shaking the monster's fangs loose from his slacks, Calum swung neatly upward and onto the roof of his house. He eased his way into a window that he had purposely not rigged for alarm, opened it and dropped to the floor. He padded along the shadows of the upstairs hall-way. Tomorrow he would deal with the dog, which continued to bark threateningly outside.

Calum caught the scent of jasmine and decided against checking Talia's room. He couldn't bear empty closets, a neat, barren room. A kitten meowed timidly from the shadows of his bedroom. Emily had no doubt forgotten one of her kittens. Calum picked up the kitten and tucked it against his body. He stroked the tiny, warm, snuggly form, and it curled into him. He would have preferred Talia doing the same, he decided whimsically. He placed it on the bed, a small comfort in the cold emptiness that enveloped him. He undressed wearily, methodically putting away his clothing. Calum glanced at his empty bed; there was no reason to fling away his clothing and hurry.

Calum slid into bed—a cold, lonely bed, except for the kitten that came snuggling close, purring. Loneliness engulfed and chilled him. He rubbed the kitten's stomach, too drained to do more than absently notice the one-o'clock cuckoo sounding from downstairs. Remnants of Talia's time at his house would surely haunt him. Just as her voice on the telephone, husky, sexy, inviting, had set him off. He'd found himself picturing what she was wearing—and dreaming of taking it off.

Calum sighed slowly and listened to the silence of his home. A silence he had preferred, pre-Talia.

A board creaked, and Talia strode into his darkened bedroom. She lowered the hair blower, raised as a weapon in her hand. "Exactly what have you done to upset my dog, Calum? Now you just go outside and make friends with poor Olaf this minute. He's insecure enough, after his previous owner's shabby treatment. By the way, you are not one of Santa's reindeer. Please don't tromp across the roof, frightening me."

Calum flipped back the blanket, then tugged it away from the hissing kitten, who had been buried. He was on his feet in one movement and striding toward her. Talia stood her ground as he slowly noted that she was wearing his chambray shirt, and that her long legs were outlined by moonlight. He noted the deep crevice in the unbuttoned front, and the pert lift of her breasts against the cloth. He wanted to toss her on his bed and ask questions later. Instead, he took the hair blower from her hand and placed it on a table.

He faced the woman who had consumed his waking and
sleeping hours. In the moonlight, Talia's hair spread across her
shoulders, gleaming like a silver mantle against his shirt. Her
eyes were huge and dark in the shadows, and her lips— She
was right where she was supposed to be, where he had left her.
A pink, fluffy rush of exhilaration swept through him. She had
waited for him . . . there were no unresolved loose ends. His
plans to keep her remained intact.

Calum reached for her and pulled her tightly against him.
He realized he was shaking. He tucked Talia's head under his
chin and, elated, smiled into her hair. She hadn't left. He tried
to push away the fear that still held him. He asked her carefully, so as not to frighten her, "Where have you been? Why
didn't you answer my messages?"

She snuggled close to him and kissed his chest. "I've been
right here, playing the busy little housekeeper. And I've been
starting a community theater, a tremendous amount of re-
warding work—mostly during the evenings, when the actors
come in from ranching. I think I've finally found my calling.
The grand opening is set for December. Elspeth has promised
that the Tallchiefs, dressed in full traditional garb, will be at
the reception. I can't wait to see you in a kilt."

For the moment, Calum bypassed the threat of wearing
Elspeth's kilt in Wyoming's notorious cold winds. He stroked
Talia's silky hair, smoothing it down her body. "You're better
than a kitten," he mused happily, and found himself grinning.

He placed his thumb beneath her chin and lifted her mouth
for a long, hard, satisfying kiss. Things weren't so bad after
all. He wallowed in a joyous jasmine-pink cloud.

"The dog… His name is Olaf…." Talia reached up to place
her arms around Calum's neck and nuzzle her face into the
curve of his throat and shoulder. "He won't stop barking until he knows I'm safe and that everything in the house is
peachy. If he wakes up the puppy, we'll spend all night trying
to get him back to sleep. The sheriff stops by and shines his
spotlight when he hears Olaf. The sheriff loves opera, and Olaf
howls when he hears a soprano."

"Can't have that," Calum agreed rawly as Talia nibbled his throat. He didn't care how the monster had come to claim his home. The dog wanted to protect Talia, just as fiercely as her brothers and father did. As Calum did. Now he understood the dog's threatening stance perfectly.

Calum frowned as the dog's excited barking continued. If Calum could just get Talia settled in his bed, everything would be fine. He wanted no spotlights, no barking dogs, no whining puppies. He didn't care how they had all come to claim his home, he just wanted to hold her close.

"Come back to bed when you've finished making friends with Olaf, darlin'."

Calum held very still, letting her invitation soak in, testing it, as Talia moved away from him. Standing by the bed, she slowly unbuttoned his shirt, dropped it to the floor and eased into the spot he had just vacated. He watched, fascinated, as she snuggled down in his bed. His heart rate wasn't the only thing to kick up. He caught a glint of gold in the moonlight. "You're wearing the ring."

She frowned at him, and stroked her finger. "I like it. I just don't like how you placed it on my finger. There I was, exhausted from belly dancing for you, fast asleep, and you slipped it on my finger. The next time you decide to do something that romantic, I want to see you coming. The Tallchief stone was a nice save."

She wore his ring. She'd waited for him. Unused to freewheeling emotions, Calum reeled at the knowledge. He knew now why people sang from rooftops. Why Duncan hurried home to Sybil every chance he had. Why flowers bloomed and birds sang.

Calum hurried through the dark house to quiet the barking dog. Olaf planted his huge paws firmly on the porch and bared his teeth, growling dangerously. Calum spoke quietly—there was the puppy and the kitten to consider. Calum didn't want Talia to be distracted tonight. "Now listen up, you black monster. This is my territory, and my woman waiting for me. Shut up and you'll get a nice juicy steak in the morning."

The dog's massive head tipped to one side and then the other, his expression one of curiosity. Calum held out his hand

and let the animal sniff it cautiously. "Okay. Give me to-night, and it's everything you want tomorrow. An insulated doghouse. The shoe of your chewing choice. A lady friend. Just don't bark. Deal?"

Olaf tried one halfhearted snarl, then plopped down on the porch, his head on his legs. Then he rolled over, belly up; it was a clear invitation. Calum crouched to rub his belly. "That's better—"

Olaf flipped to his feet and began snarling as a patrol car slid to a stop in front of Calum's house. The sheriff's spotlight pinned him. A loudspeaker broadcast an order: "Freeze. Just raise your hands and stand up."

Olaf began barking fiercely, standing with four legs locked in front of Calum's crouched nude body.

"Okay, Sheriff. You've got me." Calum slipped the huge hot-pink bow from Olaf's neck. He impatiently looped it over his aching hardness, raised his hands and stood. The sheriff's guffaws sounded immediately. Lights appeared in the house down the road as the sheriff's laughter crackled across the loudspeaker. "Naked as a jaybird, huh?"

Calum scowled at the sheriff, who slowly drove away to the radio's emotional violin music. As usual, the sheriff had forgotten to release the broadcast button on the loudspeaker. Olaf howled. A warning shot, then two, sounded from neighbors wanting sleep. A small herd of deer grazing near Calum's house took off in the moonlight. Calum held very still. *He did not want the puppy awake.* Olaf shook his massive head, ears flying, and plopped down on the porch. He whined, wanting his bribes now. Like Olaf, Calum had an immediate need, a painful one for the woman upstairs in his bed. He kept the pink bow firmly lodged low on his body and eased back into the shadows of the porch. "I know how you feel."

When Calum stepped into the room, Talia drew the quilt up to her chin. She wasn't exactly certain she was doing this right—but Calum had looked so lonely, so needing. After two long weeks away from him, she needed to hold him tight and know that he was safe. Her revenge could come later. The kitten was safely asleep on her bed, while Talia didn't feel safe at all in Calum's bed.

To claim a Tallchief could be a dangerous game. She realized the full impact of staying in his bed, waiting for him to settle the house. She realized her fear, the physical pain that would occur as she shared her body with him. Talia trembled; she wanted to claim him in a primitive way, to make him her captive, her lover. The antique ring gleamed richly in the moonlight, her bond to Calum.

Talia shivered; she wasn't certain she wanted bonds other than the psychic claiming she sought tonight. A conventional man, Calum was certain to rebel—

No doubt he wasn't happy about being caught naked on his front porch. Outlined in the faint light coming from the hallway, his body was streamlined with powerful long legs and broad shoulders that she craved to smooth. His stance, legs apart, body tense, reminded her of a warrior just back from battle and ready to be comforted by his woman. A primitive surge of pride engulfed her. She pressed her hand against the Tallchief stone. "I feel a bit like Una."

He shook his head. "What?"

Talia realized she was trembling. Calum was edgy, a violence shimmering beneath the surface. She wanted to hold him and soothe him. "You've got that warrior look, Calum Tallchief. You've been out defending the tepee, and now you're back and looking—"

"Hungry?" he asked, too softly. "You could say that." Then he turned and eased the bedroom door closed, locking it. "Let's define the ground rules right now. Why are you in my bed?"

She temporarily tossed away a lifetime of running from dominating, protective males and let the quilt slip off one shoulder. Calum responded very satisfactorily. "Talia, I want a logical explanation. If this is some kind of revenge, it's a dangerous game to play." His voice was raw and dark with hunger.

"Get into bed, Tallchief. I want to hold you, and you can tell me about Olson." She patted the empty space beside her. He looked so weary, shadows under his eyes, lines on his forehead and beside his mouth. "Oh, Calum . . ."

"I want to settle this. If I get into that bed—I can't promise—"

"To be logical? Come here. You can't settle everything to your satisfaction, at least not tonight. I have major plans." Talia ached to hold him, to soothe the tension humming through him. She looked at him sharply. "Calum, you didn't hurt Olson, did you?"

He moved through the moonlight, a tall man bound by his pride. "I don't suppose we could save the details for the morning, could we?" Then he eased over her, the quilt between them. He impatiently dismissed a froth of ruffles by her head. His hands trembled on her cheeks, and she turned to kiss them. "Why are you here, Talia, in my bed?"

Calum needed details. To forage them out and lay them neatly in a row. He needed her reassurance that everything was proceeding according to plan. Talia locked her arms around his shoulders and settled comfortably beneath him. She stroked the taut muscles rippling across his back. "Tell me how you feel, Calum. How you feel about me. I have to know."

"You want it all, don't you?"

"You could have had Kadar send me home. You didn't need to come after me."

"Oh, yes, I did," he stated firmly, his hand gently easing the quilt down until he was looking at her breasts in the moonlight. The black stone slid into the palm of his hand, just as Talia wanted to. Calum slowly covered her pale breasts with his hands and bent to kiss her. The kiss was gentle and seeking, with leashed hunger. Talia arched up to him.

Calum drew away the barrier separating them and slowly resettled between her legs. He stroked the length of her body slowly, smoothly, his hands caressing and warm down to her knees, her ankles. He kissed her shoulder, placing his hard face against her throat. Talia closed her eyes and shivered. "Calum, this is not a time for control and logic."

He chuckled against her skin. The curve of his mouth changed to a kiss, and then another. "Petrovna's rules? It's been a while. I'm trying to get the logical sequence straight. Tell me what you want."

"You."

Calum eased slowly to her side, so that they lay facing each other, their legs intertwined. His callused hand lightly skimmed her body, flowing over her rib cage to her waist and then to her hip. His fingers pressed into her softness, in a possessive gesture. The slight tremble in his hand told her how much he wanted her. She loved the heavy, rough weight of his thighs, the heated, smooth length nesting comfortably against her lower stomach. Calum drew her knee higher, smoothing her thigh and then her bottom, cupping her and rocking her gently against him. She locked her leg around his and pressed her nails slightly into his shoulder. He wasn't leaving her.

"We'll stop when you want." The dark, raw hunger in his tone reached inside her lower body and heated her.

Talia closed her eyes and bit his chin, licking its rough texture. "Good old Calum. I know I can trust you."

"Can you?" The taut male challenge caused her to open her eyes.

"Calum?" The heat in his body reached out to hers, softening it. She wanted him fiercely, wanted to ease him, to love him, to make him hers.

Calum parted her legs, gently tormented her softness, and she cried out in her desperation. "Take me, Talia. Place me where you want me," he ordered rawly, softly, tenderly, against her hot cheek.

He shivered when she first touched him, and her hand moved away from the silky sheath of heated male. She touched him again, this time firmly, caressing, marveling at his strength. Calum kissed her cheek, her eyelashes, her nose, and then sank hungrily upon her mouth. "Open for me, honey...."

She cried out, took a deep breath and placed Calum gently at the petals of her aching, tight sheath. He held very still as she squirmed beneath him, uncomfortable with the blunt, heated pressure pressing intimately against her. "This won't work."

"Okay."

"What?"

"If you say it won't work, it won't work." His heart was beating heavily against her breasts. His eyes narrowed, the moonlight drawing shadows from his lashes. Then he grinned, a careless, boyish grin that shot right into her heart.

"I worked very hard to escape a houseful of dominating, protective males, Calum Tallchief. I'm used to every possible male trick to challenge me. You're not getting away with this easy-okay business. Not now. You're years ahead of me in lovemaking, and I am determined to catch up."

Calum wrapped a strand of hair around his hand and drew her down for his kiss. "You're very hot and very tight. I don't want to hurt you. I'm not exactly in control tonight, thanks to two weeks of untangling the very neat job you did on Olson."

"Why, thank you, darlin'." Though Calum appreciated her good work, he wasn't imposing logic and schedules on her lovemaking. "I thought you said we'd stop when *I* wanted." She studied him, the seductive curve of his lower lip, the rumpled male within her web. The first lover she had ever wanted.

Lover. A jolt of heat shot through her, her lower body melting against his. "Help me."

Calum reached into the bedside stand and opened a small packet, preparing for her. Then he held her, soothed her with more kisses, until he thought he would— Calum leashed his primitive need until Talia lay warm and pliant in his arms, arching against him.

He looked at her for a very long time; she nodded, realizing that Calum was asking her permission and that she trusted him. Calum found the entrance he sought, opening her gently with his caressing fingertips, and very gently pushed deeper against the tight barrier. "Tell me to stop now, Talia."

"No. I won't." Her nails bit into his shoulder, and Talia frowned, slowly forcing them from him. "Oh. Sorry—"

Talia's flustered, hot, desperate look caused Calum to go light-headed, in contrast to the heavy desire smashing through his taut body. He smoothed a strand of hair away from her damp cheek. A sense of tender pride swept through him. "If tonight goes as I want, I expect a few small woundings. You might even decide to nibble a bit on me."

"I'll try to keep everything under control. But don't you dare stop now. It's time you knew that I'm not exactly the submissive— I'm very good at holding my own— Oh!" Her fingers pressed into his shoulders, and Una's ring gleamed in the moonlight.

Calum took her soft gasp into his mouth as he eased deeper, slowly filling her, pausing to allow her to adjust, stretching her. He lay still, his body very tense, his expression a mixture of hunger and concern and tenderness. Talia dug her nails into his shoulder. "Don't move. I hadn't expected— Oh! Oh! Calum, you can move now." Calum eased deeper, and Talia held her breath, lying very still against him.

She closed her eyes, itemized their joining and what it meant to her. She'd already known when she made her decision to make love with Calum Tallchief. She was a traditional woman in many respects, and she knew that he was the man she wanted. The man she had waited for. Calum wanted her and cared for her.

This was her decision. She could do this.

He was hers, and she cared for him. This was a commitment that was not light, because Calum was not a man to let his body rule him— She lifted her lashes to study Calum. She smoothed the taut shiver running down the length of his arm. She kissed the rigid, damp line of his jaw and knew what the effort of letting her explore her thoughts at a sensual moment had cost him. "Yes," she murmured against his mouth. "Yes."

Calum groaned shakily. "Do not move."

Good old Calum. He knew just when to toss out those challenges. Talia wrapped herself around him and rolled onto her back, drawing him over her. She nipped his shoulder, and Calum's body surged instantly, lodging fully, to the hilt. She wiggled her hips and grinned at his shocked, fierce expression. "Gotcha."

This was her fierce lover, the man she had waited for, the man who was now within her power. A gentle man, a good man, one who weighed his decisions—and he had decided on her. Her desert sheikh, her sweet little Hawk. She promised herself distantly that when she got better at this particular event and at handling Calum, she'd repay him for the Hawk's tantalizing, sensual role. Despite the uncomfortable stretching of her body, she loved his weight on her. A flowing warmth curled through her, and the tight sensation eased. She fluttered her lashes against his cheek, thanking him for his gallantry. When control was needed, she could always trust Calum. She wiggled, adjusting to the hair providing an erotic nest for her breasts. She moved her softness against him experimentally, and Calum shot a fierce, hot glance down to their bodies. Talia inhaled and chanced a curious glance downward, following his gaze. Dark and light, hard and soft, woman and man. While he studied her with a dark, intense look, she gently tightened around him.

Calum braced himself with his hands and glared down at her. "Petrovna—"

She raised her hips again and caught him. He was hers. Their kiss ignited, hot, stormy, hungry. She held him tightly, felt him deep within her, aching when he withdrew, following him, keeping him close. Calum's kiss sought hers, his heart racing against hers. Talia felt the cords in her body draw tight, keeping him, pressing him close. The rhythm of storms drew her higher, tossing her into the red-and-gold mist, and then there was only Calum . . . Calum . . .

In the flames, she turned to see their hands joined. Her pale, slender fingers, twined with his darker, larger ones. The old ring gleamed richly on her finger. *When a man of Fearghus blood places the ring upon the right woman's finger, he'll capture his true love forever. . . .* The stones were the color of blood, the pulse beating within her, the heavy, full throbbing of Calum's body locked within hers. Bloodred—the blood that came from tearing away from one life and entering another...her body torn apart and then completed... Red—the color of life, of babies fresh from their mother's nest. The Celtic design swirled like fire, flowing from the ring into Talia's body, running through her veins, heated by each brush of Calum's lips upon her parted ones. By his breath flowing upon her skin, his body withdrawing, then flowing deeply, strongly, into her raised, undulating one.

Red and gold.

Fire and heat.

Waves of fire, of exquisite pleasure...

The height of their passion startled her. Caught her on the edge of fire and heaven and burned, exploding within her.

Calum... She heard his muffled shout, her victory, her lover striding through the storms with her. Then the incredible heat, the throbbing deep within her, gently eased, and she began to drift wonderfully, warmly, down to snuggle in Calum's arms. Talia kissed his chest and clung to him, unwilling to let him move away, frightened by her emotions.

She'd always dismissed romantic entanglements. She'd just given her heart to a complex man, one who could hurt her badly. He wouldn't. She'd hold him and warm him and love him.

She hated tears. They crept from her lids to his chest, and she clung tighter. Calum had kept her safe. His heart was slowing now, his hands stroking her gently. He kissed her forehead and rocked her against him. Good old safe Calum. Her warrior. Her lover.

He tipped up her chin to lick a tear away. "I'm sorry."

She lightly tugged a whorl of hair on his chest. Here she was, Talia Petrovna, woman of the world, feeling very shy and delicate. Calum had taken very good care of her, though it had cost him, the strain showing on his intense expression. "You'd better not be sorry. You're my first lover, and I thought I did a reasonable job."

"Very reasonable," he returned, in a tone wrapped in humor and tenderness.

She dived into the tenderness, wallowed in it, as he rose to pad to the bathroom. For a musing moment, she admired his strength when hers had fled. He returned with a basin and warm water, placing it carefully beside the bed.

She sensed that what he was about to do, the cleansing of a woman newly taken by a warrior, was an unspoken, unwritten tradition of the Tallchiefs, and perhaps the Fearghus chieftains. Shy of him, Talia tried to take the damp cloth, her thighs trembling as he urged them apart with large, gentle hands. Calum eased her hands aside, indicating with the silent gesture that he had taken responsibility for their passion.

That he would tend his commitments to her. She trembled while he administered the age-old lover's ceremony, the tender cleansing, the intimate opening of her body with his fingertips, an unhurried endearment.

Tears continued to flow from her lids, dripping to dampen the pillow. Calum's tenderness, the male ceremony in which he cared for her body, had shattered her resistance. When he was finished, he placed his open hand on her stomach, smoothing it. "This was your first time."

The words were husky, running deep through his emotions. Calum's expression softened. He brought her hand to his mouth and kissed Una's ring. "Thank you, Talia . . . honey."

She bit her lip, almost crying out at the beauty of what had passed and at Calum's tenderness to her now. He studied her, smoothing her hair out upon the pillow they had shared . . . touching her lips, her throat, and skimming his open hand down her body, all the way to her toes. He caressed her arches and lightly shackled her ankles, then skimmed his hand back up to her throat. Slowly, as though he were absorbing her body into his memory by touching her, he followed her arms, tracing the feminine muscles down to her wrists. Slowly, methodically, he laced his fingers with hers, bringing their palms together. He found Una's ring and drew her hand to his lips, cherishing it with an intricate, tantalizing, erotic design of kisses. Then he turned her palm to his mouth, treating it just as carefully, just as intimately.

"Thank you," he whispered again, and this time the moonlight ran silvery and damp across his lashes.

She touched his cheek. "I missed you, Calum."

"I missed you, too, honey." Calum eased slowly down beside her, pulling up the quilt to cover them.

When she lay against him, he held her close. "It won't hurt that way again. We'll wait, and you can choose the next—"

Her finger, resting upon his lips, stilled the rest of his sentence. She gathered him close and safe and Talia sighed against his chest. She'd waited two long weeks to have him in her clutches; the sound of his deep voice on the telephone the first week had been too much. She draped a leg over him and snuggled closer. The dark, stormy edges of Calum Tallchief had gently settled, for a time. She knew then why Tallchief Lake reminded her of Calum—the smooth calm covering deep currents that, when lashed by the elements, could rise into a torrent of white, fearsome waves.

Perhaps Una had sensed that about the Sioux chieftain who had captured her. That beneath the warrior's stoic arrogance, emotions ran deep and true, emotions that a woman could cling to. Talia sensed that she knew Una very well, that when the warrior calmed, he needed care and tenderness, and that his allegiance ran deep. Perhaps Tallchief had tended Una, just as Calum had cared for Talia's newly opened body.

She inhaled unsteadily, fiercely joyful that she had kept herself for this moment, when intimacy was treasured by a man she adored.

He'd just called her *honey*, an endearment. Calum wasn't the sort of man to issue endearments on a regular basis to every woman. She hugged that comfort deep in her heart.

She lifted slightly to find her captive sleeping deeply. A masculine contrast sprawled across the ruffled pillow shams and flowery printed sheets, Calum looked carefree and vulnerable. Talia inhaled deeply, wallowing in her victory. She ran her foot slowly down her captive's hair-roughened shin, fondly patted his firm rear, and settled down to sleep in his arms.

Eight

Before dawn, Talia crouched in the kitchen with the kitten and the puppy. They required regular small feedings, and had just been fed and were settling down to sleep. The regular sound of Olaf's claws on the front porch had continued all through the feeding, the dog patrolling his territory until the house settled. Olaf had acted slightly jealous of the puppy and the kitten, though he seemed pleased when they frolicked over him and between his paws. He didn't grumble when they tugged on his ears, just lifted his jowls in a doggy grin.

Because Olaf needed to know that he hadn't been displaced, Talia took special care to open the door and speak quietly to him. She absently noted his pink bow, looped over the doorknob. She tossed him a doggy biscuit and padded back through the living room.

She glimpsed a movement in the dark kitchen, then Calum moved through the shadows and scooped her up in his arms. Talia cuddled against him, instantly alerted to his aroused body beneath her hips. He held her tightly against him, his expression fierce and stark. His heart pounded heavily against her breast, as though he had just run a gauntlet of torture.

Talia had no doubt that Tallchief had looked just as fierce when he claimed Una. She knew how Una must have felt, the feminine tenderness of a woman welcoming the man she had chosen. A woman's choice, that of balancing her mind and her body. To select her lover was the ultimate choice. She smoothed the hard planes of his chest and placed her palm over his racing heart. For all his calm and steel, Calum had been frightened when he awoke and found her gone. He'd reacted instinctively, seeking her out and holding her.

Talia placed her arms around his shoulders and stroked the taut muscles of his neck. She saw then the pain that Calum covered so well; it hummed through him like a vibrating wire. Pain brought by the sudden loss of his parents and by his wife's death. "I'm not going anywhere, Calum. Except back to bed."

"*Mine.*" The statement was flat, arrogant, possessive, and yet a vulnerable uncertainty lurked beneath it. A man who liked things completed, he would want her by his side in the morning. And that was exactly where she wanted to awake, taking equal responsibility for her actions. However, the warrior technique would not suffice in daylight. She'd allow him the night.

She placed her hand on his jaw, caressing him softly. His head went up a notch, an arrogant warrior tilt to it. Calum and Olaf were more alike than she had first thought. Both lonely, battle-scarred warriors, wary of a tender hand.

Talia held Calum closer. He needed her. Talia kissed the damp side of his throat and cuddled closer. She gently bit his shoulder, then licked the small wound, and Calum relaxed slightly. For a time, Calum was her very own.

He carried her up the stairs and placed her carefully upon his bed. She smoothed the flowery sheets, this nest she had prepared for them. When she opened her arms to him, Calum gently eased down upon her. Talia ached for him; she intimately adjusted her body beneath his and took him gently, slowly, inside her. Calum trembled, then went very still. The tension humming through him frightened her . . . yet she clung to him, soothed him, spattering tiny kisses on his hard fore-head, his glossy straight lashes and jutting cheekbones.

Calum gave himself up to her hard, fast kiss, moving in-stinctively deeper within her, burying himself possessively.

He withdrew slightly and Talia looked at him.

"Tonight changes everything, honey. I'm upping the ante." The arrogance returned, mixed with tenderness, as Calum lowered himself again, resting very deep within the throbbing warmth of her. He kissed her hungrily, scooping her hips in his palms and lifting her high as he moved, very slow, very con-trolled, against her. She didn't have time to think about what had changed or what ante had been raised as Calum gathered her closer, making her a part of him.

Then Calum bent his mouth to her ear, kissed it and began to tell her how he felt, close and tight within her. Talia's blush deepened, her body straining against his hard one, as she found the rhythm of the dark, powerful storms, the urgency of Calum's raw, deep tone taking her higher. He was her war-rior, her lover, taking, giving, tantalizing. She held him tight and flung herself into his keeping.

Later, when they had burst together and drifted slowly back to reality, Calum carried her into the shower and treated her just as gently as the first time. She was too tired to do any-thing but move into the shelter of his arms.

The morning sun crossing into the room awakened her. Talia hugged the night to her; here in this flowery garden was the male she had captured and brought to her lair. An admirable trophy, one she had waited for on a primitive level. Instincts, thought Talia. Marvelous, good, old-fashioned instincts. He looked delectable against the mauve flowery print sheets and the ruffled pillow shams she had added to his bed. Since she had been sleeping in it, she'd wanted to feel comfortable, and she'd never liked Calum's sterile white sheets. He lay sprawled on his side, his arm and a heavy thigh crossing hers posses-sively, his morning beard darkening his strong jaw. His usu-ally neatly clipped hair had grown shaggy, gleaming blue-black against his dark skin. A dark mat of hair covering his chest veed downward, and Talia inhaled as Calum's body began to change.

His drowsy gray eyes opened slowly, and a sensual curve replaced his usually grim mouth. "What you see is what you get," he drawled huskily.

Startled, Talia jerked up the sheet, tugged it away and wrapped her body in it. She walked shakily to the bathroom. She wasn't quite ready to deal with Calum in a playful mood just yet.

He'd changed the rules, she decided as she showered, needing privacy.

Calum Tallchief had changed the rules and the schedule. She would have to watch him very carefully. She knew full well how Petrovna males dominated and protected their women, and she wouldn't let Calum take her freedom.

She reached for a towel and caught the glitter of Una's garnets—*When a man of Fearghus blood places the ring upon the right woman's finger, he'll capture his true love forever.*

Talia carefully removed the ring. She knew herself too well. She resented day-to-day living, the kind needed to forge a strong relationship. She resented domineering and traditional men who occasionally acted like warriors, claiming their rights.

Tonight changes everything.... I'm upping the ante....

"I am not acting miffed, Elspeth." Calum tracked Talia with his frown. She moved easily among his entire family, serving them breakfast with ease. Calum tried not to notice her graceful saunter, the sway of her hips that was like no other woman's. "Just because a whole horde of Tallchiefs land on my doorstep my first morning home, *why should I be miffed?*"

She flushed as she glanced at him and looked away suddenly. Calum cursed silently. Talia needed his reassurance that he hadn't taken her lightly; she needed to be cuddled and cherished.

Calum the cool—his nickname taunted him.

He glared at the family he loved; an infestation of Tallchief males and accompanying females, along with Olaf, an unnamed puppy and kitten and Duncan's huge wolf dog, Thorn, prevented him approaching Talia on a romantic level.

He had awakened amid flowery sheets and ruffles and had stepped into a shower scented of Talia, allowing him to prolong the new softness in his life a bit longer. The feminine clutter across his bathroom counter had fascinated him. He'd picked up a lacy bra drying on the towel rack and run his fingers over it, dreaming of softer fare.

Why had she taken off Una's ring?

The ring had gleamed when they first made love, as though loving made the colors richer, forging them in red and gold. Calum's body hardened painfully as he remembered Talia's uneven, soft cries, the delicate pulsing of her body tight around him, flowing beneath him.

He cursed silently. He was a traditional man after all, slightly proud that his woman had held her body for him, that he had taken her— Calum realized that his thoughts were not politically correct; nor were they those of a contemporary male. When terms like *maiden-shield* dropped into a man's mind, he definitely needed to update himself.

Talia placed a glass filled with *biscotti* on the table. Her breast touched the nape of Calum's neck, and his lower body lurched with a painful reminder of how he had hoped to spend the morning. In bed with Talia, sorting out the logical flow of their relationship.

They'd known each other one month.

He still didn't trust her to drop her revenge on Olson so easily.

Talia probably had an alternate plan in effect right now. He was off balance, sensuously hungry, and uncertain. Calum detested the combination of emotions disrupting his life. He simply wanted Talia back in his arms, back in his bed and committed to him.

He realized with slight distaste that greed had just stepped into his life.

Calum scowled at the kitten nestled against Talia's body. He knew instinctively that when plans went into motion before they were fully developed, anything could go awry.

Logically, he should have been the one to initiate their love-making last night. He followed Talia's path to pick up the whining puppy, tracing the sway of her hips; he resented this knowledge that the moment of seduction, and therefore the commitment he wanted to get from Talia, had been taken away from him.

Talia had claimed him before the ground-level foundation of commitments and promises had been properly laid.

Laid. The word dropped like a stone upon him. He had been laid, well and good. Drawn into a flowery bed of ruffles and jasmine and— He realized he was scowling. Talia just... counted coup, Calum decided darkly in terms of his Sioux chieftain grandfather.

A modern woman, she had taken the initiative in their love-making. While he appreciated her need of him, Calum realized darkly that he was old-fashioned and needed the courting stage.

Roles. Male-female. Ceremony. He wanted ceremony and courtship and a long-term relationship with Talia. She could easily bolt when faced with restrictions of a conventional relationship.

Olaf padded after Talia, eager for a petting, reminding Calum of himself. The comparison grated at him.

He rummaged back through time, to his needs in his marriage. They had been starkly devoid of the tenderness he felt for Talia.

From the drift of the conversation when he arrived downstairs, Talia had invited his family for breakfast. An impromptu affair to which Sybil brought an apple pie and Elspeth brought freshly baked bread. Duncan had placed a gallon jar of creamy cow's milk on the counter.

Talia periodically unscrewed the container, dipped her finger into the cream and sucked it. Calum inhaled sharply, suddenly aware of how much he wanted her. He jerked out his only defense. "I do not like flowery sheets or ruffles."

The Tallchiefs' black heads jerked in his direction. Calum glared at Talia, who lifted her eyebrows.

Duncan looked amused, Sybil hid a grin, and Elspeth's lips curved softly. Birk cheerfully slid into the too-quiet void. "I've been here every morning. Had to. You should appreciate the new greenhouse I built onto your house. Talia says fresh herbs are the best and you require the very best." Birk bit into a chocolate *biscotto* and washed it down with vanilla-flavored coffee. He grinned blithely at Calum, who scowled back. "Every good housekeeper needs an indoor herb garden. She's ready to start making flavored vinegars—says there's a real lack of them in Amen Flats."

Calum almost winced at the "housekeeper" remark. His family had accepted Talia. But she had placed Una's ring aside.

In the cheery buttercup-yellow kitchen softened by woven cotton rugs, Talia settled like a butterfly against the counter. She contemplated Calum over the puppy, who was licking at her chin. With a braid of garlic and chili peppers on the wall next to her, Talia looked very Slavic and very cool.

She had given herself to him. The thought stunned him. Uneasily, he studied her expression. It was the look of a satisfied, victorious cat who had just caught the mouse she wanted. Calum's trickle of uneasiness rose up the nape of his neck.

As the flow of the Tallchiefs continued around him, Calum began to hate cute, cuddly, lovable puppies and kittens. He didn't remove his gaze from Talia. She was too quiet.

She wore a single braid and her knee-high boots, and she was dressed in black. The typical ready-for-action Talia costume. Olaf grinned up at her. The phone had rung multiple times this morning. While Duncan discussed the family's cattle business with The Tallchiefs, Calum had noted darkly that most of Talia's calls were from single males. From her comments, Calum also noted that Talia's play, *Nachos and Nanette,* needed work before presentation. His experience as a substitute reviewer told him that, even in rural Amen Flats, she'd be cut to ribbons. To protect Talia, he decided to watch rehearsals and offer his help. He wanted to be a supportive mate.

He wouldn't have anyone booing his bride.

"By the way, Calum the cool..." Elspeth said softly, firmly. He stopped his report on family investments to listen to Talia speaking on the phone. Elspeth continued, amused by her brother's distraction. "I'm not clipping your hair again."

Duncan and Sybil shared a tender look. Though Elspeth cared carefully for her brothers, she renounced care of them when she believed the right woman was at hand. Sybil leaned to kiss Duncan, Megan sleeping safely in his arms.

Then Duncan's sea-gray gaze slowly turned to Calum. "Have you picked out a spot on the mountain, Calum?"

Calum hesitated, fearing that Talia might feel too constricted by the knowledge that his family expected him to claim her. According to her file, Talia had no problems leaving a situation that did not suit her. He needed time to make himself enticing. A month was not time enough for her to know his best selling points or for him to offer marriage in a romantic way—where *he* had the advantage of choosing the moment of seduction. He tried a diversion. "How is the women's center going, Sybil? I know Lacey and you have been helping."

"What spot on Tallchief Mountain?" Talia's question plopped out into the brightly furnished kitchen.

"I'll explain later." Calum realized with horror that he had just flushed. As boys, the Tallchiefs had planned to set up their family tepees on the mountain. Duncan had snatched the past and tossed it at Calum with a grin. Calum trembled a bit when Talia dipped into the cream again and sucked her finger. "I thought you might want to ride with me this morning."

"Uh . . ." Talia went very still. Her blush was a contrast to her wide-eyed innocent look. "Actually, I'm a little stiff this morning—from my new yoga exercises. I've got the house-keeping to do, and the play in the afternoon. I'll have to hurry—"

Calum got very slowly to his feet. He'd hurt her last night, and now the barricades were going up. Any minute, she'd be packing. He rubbed the back of his taut neck and glared at her. The cuckoo he hadn't seen yet sounded ten times. It set off the sound alarms he had automatically turned on when he came downstairs.

While his family burst out laughing, Calum walked stiffly to the alarm box and punched in the disconnect code. He caught a scent of jasmine, remembered the fragrances and feminine clutter in his bathroom and knew that he wanted anything Talia wanted. "Fine."

Then he walked to her, drew her into the scented sanctuary of herbs and kissed her. Talia wilted afterward, cuddling comfortably against him. His fears ebbed and eased. She was where she was supposed to be. She ran her fingers through his hair, and he fell into the soft blue depths of her eyes. "Everything will be just fine, Calum. I know you need reassurance. I'm sorry I'm not experienced at morning-afters. You won't have to worry about that again."

Making sense of Talia's statement cost him the better part of the day. He'd repeated Talia's "won't have to worry about that again" statement out loud to find the baseline in it. Did that mean she wasn't going to bed with him again?

From his experience, it was best to move swiftly, effectively, upon differing bargaining points. For that reason, he had spent the morning and early afternoon clearing his work calendar and referring clients to another corporate bird dog. He checked the budget for the women's shelter and the Tallchief family accounts for which he was responsible. He wanted everything running smoothly, so that he'd have the entire winter to hook Talia, to lay aside her fears that he was a boring nerd and that a marriage with him was reasonable and not overly structured or confining.

In the socks Talia had sloshed with bleach, he padded out to examine his formerly sterile and quiet home. Talia had left his streamlined office alone, but the rest of the house blended herbs and Native American rugs and throws, and she had carefully arranged the memories of his past throughout the house. There were newly framed pictures of Duncan's family, as well as an antique copper water heater filled with a huge bouquet of eucalyptus and dried wildflowers. Antique jars caught the day's light in tints of blue and purple. Candles of every scent, shape and color lurked in unpredictable places. A Cheshire cat pillow sat on his modern staircase, grinning at him.

His former starkly modern home had a pleasantly cluttered look, a warm look that said *home*.

Olaf had seemed abandoned when Talia left for her busy day, so Calum had let him into the house. The big dog padded at his side, a friend in a newly cluttered world. He howled as the cuckoo leaped out of its walnut house and baited him repeatedly. Because the kitten and the puppy were crying, Calum picked one up in each hand and tucked them close to his body. They quieted after a few sniffs at his scorched shirt, and together they all set off to discover Talia's creation.

For a moment, Calum had stood riveted in his living room, bound by a creative festival of colors and nostalgia. The Tall-chief branded board hung above the mantel, the leather-sheathed hunting knife hanging from it by leather thongs. Comfortable pillows spattered the couch and ranged onto the floor. He approached his rearranged bookshelves carefully. Talia's how-to books and cookbooks spread across an entire shelf.

Laundry spilled from the utility room into the hallway. Calum's shirts hung from a rack, a mass of scorched wrinkles. He touched the scorched imprint of an iron lightly. The mark, shared by the one on his collar, was endearing.

Calum had taken an assortment of telephone messages for Talia, fed Olaf, the puppy and the kitten and quickly made a pasta salad for Talia's lunch. He also wanted to be prepared in case he could manage to get her upstairs or downstairs or in the kitchen. He was just fantasizing about the kitchen table when Talia breezed in, laden with groceries.

For all his plans for step-by-step action, Calum grabbed her, lifted her to the countertop and placed his hands flat on the counter by her hips. "What do you mean, I won't have to worry about *that* again?" he demanded.

Talia smoothed the ironed wrinkles covering his chest. "Your glasses are tipped and steamed, and you're upset. Goodness, darlin', you can look so fierce."

"*Upset* is an understatement. What did you mean, Talia?" Calum placed his glasses aside.

He closed his eyes while Talia gently soothed the bridge of his nose, where the glasses had left marks. "Calum, you really are a fragile person. You're off balance because I . . . well, I had you last night."

Her assessment was accurate and nettled him. He caught her left hand and brought it to his mouth. "That's debatable. Why aren't you wearing my ring?"

"Because..." Talia took a deep breath and set her chin. "It's not logical. The ring is meant for a true love, Calum. Not for the object of a man who has just discovered that his life is missing—" she flushed before going on "—certain creature comforts."

Calum narrowed his eyes. "Translation—you mean a nerd who has just discovered sex."

"You're terribly old-fashioned, Calum." She held up a finger to stop his next argument. "You will not offer to pay me for housekeeping. We're on a fine line here, and if my family found out you were paying me *and* sleeping with me, they would be offended. *I* would be offended. It isn't wise, in the employer-employee sense of the word. The Petrovnas would have to have revenge. I couldn't protect you."

She paused and smoothed his taut jaw. "By the way, thank you for reuniting Roy and Jan. My sister called me. That was a neat piece of cupid craftsmanship...sending romantic notes to Jan and to Roy and gradually explaining Olson's part. How did you know that Roy wouldn't confront Olson?"

Calum had approached Roy cautiously, and together they had decided that Olson's scorned wife could better exact justice. Calum dismissed everyone else but Talia. He tilted his head, his mind reeling from Talia's verbal curveball. "Let me get this straight. *You* are using logic?"

"Basically. Just general deduction stuff. Sorry about the plumbing in the downstairs bathroom. They're not making pipes and wrenches like they used to." Talia hopped off the counter. She flicked a glance down at his jeans. "Calum, you should wear your jeans longer. Above-the-ankle length doesn't do anything for you."

Calum ran his hands through his hair, hesitated with growing fear, and followed her look. His jeans, dotted by white bleached spots, were at high-nerd level.

Talia patted Olaf and gave him a treat. "He reminds me of you, Calum."

Calum studied the big, scarred dog briefly. "I don't know why." Then he moved toward Talia, and so did Olaf.

Talia turned to him slowly. "Calum, I'm moving to Lacey's house—"

"What?" He stared at her, ready to pluck her up and run with her. This was the day after the night she'd given herself to him— Calum reeled at the dark anger enfolding him.

She began quickly unpacking the groceries. "She's remodeling that old bordello and has lots of room. She needs me."

Calum stood very still. His world was crumbling, and he couldn't find the right words to stop Talia from leaving him. He really wanted the tender option of gentle persuasion. *"She* needs you?"

Talia's hands shook as she avoided facing him. Calum took small comfort in the fact that she wasn't as cool as she seemed. His heart was racing as though he were fighting for his life. Maybe he was. "Stand and fight, Talia. You're up to it," he said, very quietly.

She turned to face him, her expression serious. "This isn't a showdown, Calum. We both could lose."

Calum took her face in his hands and lifted it to his. "Take a chance, honey. Take it with me."

A tear dropped onto his thumb as Talia closed her lashes. "Calum, we're so opposite. I'm an extreme person. You like to think things through. Or sometimes you do. You are very methodical, Calum Tallchief. It's frightening."

"You're afraid of me, is that it?"

Her eyes opened. "Absolutely not. There are times, though, that I'd like to demolish you."

"So stay and do it."

"That sounds suspiciously like a challenge, Calum. You like neat packages, and I don't. I could demolish you easily."

"Just try it." Then he placed his lips on hers and folded her body against his. Calum tucked his chin over the top of her head and stroked her tense body. He noted that Talia did not relax easily against him, but held herself slightly apart.

Nine

Talia gripped the rock face with her gloved fingertips, pitting her strength against Tallchief Mountain. She needed the challenge to exorcise the tension humming through her, tension caused by one Calum Tallchief. She tested her safety rope, attached to nails hammered into the red rock surface of the cliff. The wind howled around the iced rock, buffeting her. "Stand and fight," she muttered as a pebble bounced downward, forcing her to huddle against the rock face. "Is this the OK Corral or what?"

She pounded a stake into the rock and attached her safety line to it. Calum wasn't easy game. So what? She'd always liked challenges. So why had she been crying? Talia swallowed the tight emotion in her throat. She'd actually fallen asleep in a tiny cave, exhausted from the emotions that Calum managed to drag out of her.

She eased her climbing boot slowly to one side, found a secure ledge and placed her weight on it. A snowflake slid down her cheek, and another landed on her nose. She inhaled the freezing air, savoring it, and inched higher on the rock face. Her up-to-date gear and clothing kept the cold at bay.

Extreme exercise had always helped her think better. Yesterday, Calum had cost her three male actors just by sitting in the theater during practice and glowering at them. *Nachos and Nanette* was her first play; he shouldn't have propped his boots on the chair in front of him, crossed his arms over his chest and snorted at every beautifully sculpted punch line.

She'd decided not to embarrass him in front of his friends, saving her thoughts for later. Calum had stuffed her into her coat and walked her home. His hand on the back of her waist, guiding her across the street, and the way he shielded the cutting mid-November wind from her, had made it clear that she was his woman. She resolved that, as a contemporary woman, she shouldn't have been so grateful for his tall body blocking the wind. But then, she had always suffered from periodic bouts of self-preservation.

When he'd opened the door, delicious food scents ensnared her. One look at the candles, the flowers, the lit fireplace and the expensive wine and she had backed against the wall. The beautifully wrapped gift by the flowers had looked ominous and threatening to her freedom. She had caught Calum's dark, determined and wary look and run for her room and locked the door.

Talia breathed deeply, aware that sunshine no longer warmed the unrelenting rock. An expert climber, she jerked down her knit mask and readjusted her goggles. "Stand and fight. Is that a thing to say to a lady?"

She muttered the African elephant-dung curse. Of course Calum would know how to challenge her; she hadn't found how to challenge him.

Rocks dislodged under one foot and bounced down the cliff. Talia eased higher, then pounded another nail into the flat red rock surface. She tested it, and when it held, she began to inch upward.

Just one sultry look from his smoke-gray eyes and she began to melt. Thoughts of him had probably caused her slide down thirty feet of sheer rock earlier, her safety line and a friendly root saving her.

She wasn't meant for small towns and family men who held gray-eyed, black-haired Tallchief babies. Beautiful antique rings with legends of lovers weren't her style; she wore dynamic modern jewelry. She panicked when she thought of committing to Calum Tallchief.

This morning, Calum Tallchief had worn the stone around his throat, nettling Talia. When she arrived in the kitchen, he had been flipping pancakes expertly, dressed in worn jeans and nothing else. Every instinct Talia possessed had told her to go to him and lay him upon the kitchen table, to feast upon him.

She sniffed the cold air, scented with Tallchief Mountain pines and fresh earth. She'd never stayed in one place too long, and the longer she stayed in the Tallchief home nest, the more difficult it would be to leave.

A rock came loose in her hand and skittered down the face of the cliff. Talia's elephant-dung curse hit the icy wind. She couldn't trust Calum. He hadn't said anything when she infiltrated his computer system. He didn't seem to mind the feminine clutter in his bathroom; she'd been certain that would unnerve him. "There is no explaining him sometimes. Unorganizing his closet was a piece of art," she stated breathlessly.

A blast of winter wind hit her, flattening her against the cold surface. Talia glanced at the clouds that were bringing darkness sooner than she had planned. Her boot found a rock; it dislodged when she placed her weight upon it. Sleet began pelting her, and Talia realized that she had to reach the top of the cliff quickly. Apparently the weather on Tallchief Mountain was just as volatile as one Calum Tallchief.

Her fingers slipped, numbed by the sudden cold temperatures. She realized that she'd been running on anger and on nerves caused by Calum.

He had "possessive, traditional male" written all over him, and that was a commodity she'd avoided for a lifetime.

A fresh blast of sleet iced on the rock, and her glove slipped away. Talia realized with horror that she had thoughtlessly placed herself in danger. The cold penetrated layers of clothing and silk underwear now, and her fingers were too numb to grip properly. The safety line had iced, and a mixture of sleet and snow pounded her. Her sleepless night and her exhaustion had taken the last of her resources. Her nap had consumed precious time. She flattened against the iced wall and began searching for shelter, a small niche like the one she had napped in.

If she couldn't find shelter in which to rest, she would continue scaling the cliff. Survival training would serve her once she was in the pines, and then she would make her way down easily after the sun warmed the rock. She glanced at the forbidding late-afternoon sky and knew that Tallchief Mountain could be enclosed in a winter storm for days.

Someone would miss her; a big SOS or a bonfire would draw attention to her. . . .

A pebble dislodged from above her, and above the howling wind, she heard Calum yell, "Petrovna, I'm getting tired of waiting for you!"

Talia gripped the rock face tightly; her heart raced. She leaned back carefully to look upward. "Calum?"

Against the cloudy sky, he loomed over the top of the cliff, his legs braced wide and his hands resting on his hips. Hail pounded his worn Western hat and bounced off his shoulders, which were covered by a warm shearling jacket. He began swirling a lariat against the gray, stormy sky. "Come on, Petrovna. Don't be difficult. Just take the rope and make it easy for the both of us."

"This is my gig, Tallchief. Who invited you?"

"You did, precious." His tone was too confident. She decided not to ask the when and how of her invitation to him.

From her precarious position, she tossed him a reminder that she wasn't precious or sweet. "So how do you like your closet, Tallchief?"

"It's a real piece of art, Petrovna. I like ties wrapped around my mismatched sock-balls. Now take the damn rope and haul it up here fast." The rope dropped neatly by her side, his order impatient.

Talia closed her eyes; coated in ice and clinging by her fingertips from a sheer cliff, she had no option but to accept his command. To salve her pride, she tossed out her best comeback. "I resent your tone, Tallchief. You cost me three of my best actors. It's not that easy to find men who will cooperate and wear tights in this town, you know. And I did *not* write a boring play. *Nachos and Nanette* is a highly sophisticated comedy with a deep, heart-wrenching message. Just how did you get up here?''

"I took the horse trail, city girl."

"Of course, a horse trail. I knew that." Reluctantly Talia agreed that she hadn't been wise to approach the cliff on Tallchief Mountain in the face of a winter storm. She resented being the object of Calum's rescue and that she had no choice but to take the rope, inserting her foot into the loop he had prepared. She grabbed the rope to wrap it around her waist and tugged the line twice; the rope drew her slowly, carefully, up the side of the cliff. Talia used her chilled hands and feet to grasp rocks and roots; she eased onto the top ledge and grasped . . . Calum's worn Western boot. She stared up at him as his hands went under her arms; he lifted her easily to safety and tugged off her iced goggles.

She'd forgotten his strength; when they made love, he'd been so gentle— He stood back, his collar turned up against the wind, his hands on his hips, his legs braced apart. He looked as much a part of Tallchief Mountain as the rocks and the pines and the snowcapped mountains beyond.

She stared at the rain freezing to his black beard; the clean-cut Calum she knew shaved twice daily. Slowly she met the cold, steely glint of his eyes, shadowed by his hat. A trickle of fear slid up her spine. This was the real Calum Tallchief— dark, stormy, dangerous. This would be the side of him that his parents' murderer had seen that night, civilization stripped away. Calum looked like an old-West gunfighter, a well-worn revolver strapped to his jeaned thigh. His eyes cut coldly down her black-clad body. "You looked like a damn ninja crawling up the face of that cliff. Are you all right?"

"I'm just fine." She was lying; her muscles ached, her body was frozen and trembling from fear and exhaustion. Now she faced a towering, angry cowboy who looked about as warm as the cold rock face of the cliff. A short distance away, his horse stood with the rope attached to its saddle horn. She noted that the horse was not the elegant Arabian, which was probably

related to Kadar's, but rather a seasoned cow horse used in a
rodeo.

"Gee, that felt great. It's a great day for—" she managed
lightly before he scooped her up in his arms and loped through
the hail to a tepee settled in the pines. His strength startled her
again; she remembered the Desert Hawk's easy control of her.

Calum deposited her none too gently upon a thick bedding
of sleeping bags, furs and blankets. "Okay, city girl. You've
had your fun. Now get your clothes off and get into that bed.
You'd better be in it when I get back."

Talia studied the interior of the tepee. "At least you haven't
murdered any animals to make this. Imagine, insulating canvas with— She took one look at his grim, dangerous expression and decided that getting into bed was just what she wanted
to do. She sat up and began to strip away her gloves. Her
numbed fingers caused her to be clumsy, and Calum cursed
darkly. He ripped away his leather gloves, crouched in front of
her and began unlacing her climbing boots. He grimly stripped
away her clothing, extracted warm rocks from the sleeping bag
and stuffed her into it. She decided now was not the time for
chitchat, and attempted a friendly smile.

Calum scowled back at her, tugged his hat lower and jerked
on his gloves before leaving.

Talia examined the tepee, which was protected by boughs
layered around it. Smoke rose in the center of the tepee, drifting around the blackened pot over the fire, and an ancient
coffeepot sat on a flattened rock; the flowers were frostbitten
and wilted, and the elegantly wrapped package of last night
was battered slightly. An unopened bottle of wine sat near
scented candles.

Calum entered in a gust of sleet and snow. He tossed the
saddle and tack into a corner, ripped off his hat and expertly
sailed it to rest on the saddle horn. The gloves followed, and
then his coat. He secured the tent flap, crouched by the fire and
warmed his hands near it. He continued to ignore Talia while
he ladled soup into a bowl and poured coffee into a steel cup.
Talia studied the tense muscle contracting in his jaw and decided to let him open the conversation. She tugged the sleeping bag up to her chin.

But, since waiting ran against her nature, she decided to open with a tentative, prim, safe "Thank you, Calum."

He snorted, looked at her and shook his head. He handed the soup to her, a thick, delicious clam chowder, and the mug of coffee. Then he sat, stripped off his revolver, wrapping it expertly in the gun belt, and placed it aside. He began eating his meal, ignoring her.

She decided to open with a compliment, a silence-softener. "The chowder was absolutely delicious. Thank you, Calum."

"Leftovers." His single word reminded her of the beautiful meal he had prepared the previous night.

"Leftovers are always good."

He grunted. She decided she was making progress. There was the possibility she could pacify his unjustified bristling. "Is the horse cozy?"

He stared at her as if she'd asked how the tropical storm was doing outside. "Just peachy."

Talia hitched up the cloth that had slipped from her bare shoulder. She tucked it under her chin and began undoing her damp single braid, spreading her hair around her shoulders to dry.

"Petrovna..." Calum's tone held amusement. "We're lovers, remember?"

"I wouldn't exactly say we're lovers, darlin'," she managed to drawl carelessly as Calum began to draw off his boots. She watched, fascinated, as he cleared away dinner and arranged her clothing to dry.

Towering over her, his rugged face and beard lit by the fire, Calum looked down at her. "Feel like talking? What made you decide to try to climb Tallchief Mountain with a storm brewing?"

"You upset me." To her mortification, she began to cry.

"*I* upset *you*," Calum muttered darkly.

Talia dashed away the tears dripping from her cheeks. "Thank you, Calum Tallchief. I haven't cried since I was eighteen, and see what you've done." She flung out a hand helplessly. "Get into that bed, you said—just like you had the right to say it in that way. You don't."

Calum's hands stopped unbuttoning his wool shirt. He glowered down at her. "The hell I don't. You're my woman, Talia. The only one to make me mad enough to... Okay, so I'm not into spanking, but watching you slide down an ice wall for a good thirty or forty feet before you snagged that root and your safety line caught you? About then, I wanted to put that cute fanny over my knee and paddle you like Fiona needed as a child."

"*I would not like that, Calum Middle-Name Tallchief.*"

"*Like?*" The word was fired back at her, as though shot from a six-gun. "Now get this, Petrovna. When a man sees the woman he *loves* acting like an idiot on a dangerous, icy cliff, he starts thinking all sorts of things. For one—he'd like to have a life with her... a safe one, maybe with kids. He'd like to see her grow old and—" Calum ran his fingers through his hair, then he began undressing grimly. "We'll talk about this when we both settle down."

Love? Talia sniffed and dried her tears. She'd taken him so deeply into her body, until she felt she'd burst with the fullness of him—*and she didn't even know if he had a middle name.* Lit by the firelight, Calum's face was weary and hard, lines deep across his forehead. "I don't know that I'm up to that love part," she stated carefully. "Even if I were, you shouldn't have flung it at me like an old shoe."

"Move over." Calum, stripped down to his boxer shorts, slid into the sleeping bag with her. She eased to the limits of the bag, away from him. He folded his arms behind his head and stared at the smoke drifting through the top of the tepee. "Go to sleep."

"Calum, you're acting overly emotional."

He snorted and continued to stare at the smoke. "A climber died four years ago in weather situations just like this. He came down like a rag doll."

"You were afraid for me." Talia placed her hand on his chest, surprised that his heart raced beneath her palm. "You're still afraid."

"I've been afraid before. Go to sleep." He glanced impatiently at her and wiped away a tear from her cheek. "You look like hell, Petrovna, all big-eyed, and your hair—" He gently lifted a strand away from her cheek and placed his hand on her head, rubbing her scalp with his fingertips.

Talia turned her head to look at him. "Why do you do that?"

Calum's rugged yet whimsical expression fascinated Talia. "You're touchable, Petrovna. You respond instantly. You actually purr."

"That's ridiculous. You make me sound like a cat—"

"Kitten. A soft, cuddly kitten. One that I want to hold very much." The tenderness in Calum's expression ensnared her.

"Are you asking?" she asked when she could manage a breathless whisper. She really hoped he was asking.

"Come here, honey. Let me hold you." Calum's expression was wary and vulnerable, yet he made no more moves to take her into his arms. He was leaving that choice to her.

Talia needed his arms around her. She pushed aside her fears of being hurt and slid into his arms. He eased aside her hair, and Talia carefully placed her head upon his shoulder. Calum tucked the sleeping bag up tight to her chin and rocked her gently. He exhaled slowly, and she realized that he had been waiting for her to choose him, holding his breath out of fear that she wouldn't. Talia stroked the hair on his chest and settled more heavily against his solid body. She looked at the flames, gave herself to his warmth and safety and began to relax.

The wind howled outside, and Calum stroked her hair, nuzzling her forehead periodically with tiny, comforting kisses. "Better?"

She nodded slowly and closed her eyes, the fight for her survival ebbing away from her tense muscles. In the next instant, Calum sat up, ripped away the sleeping bag and studied her body. Flattened on the bedding, with her hands covering her breasts and lower, Talia glared up at him. "Don't you dare."

Calum's broad shoulders rippled in the firelight as his hands moved slowly, expertly, over her body. "Now is no time to play doctor," she muttered when he studied her from head to toe, found the slight scrapes on her knees and spread antiseptic on them. She noted the quick, efficient way he applied adhesive bandages and an automatic healing kiss. "You've done this before."

He covered her with the sleeping bag, then tossed wood on the fire. "Fiona's knees and elbows, on a regular basis," he explained curtly. "I knew you wouldn't let me look until you were relaxed and not on the defensive. You are a very defensive lady, Talia. You let me come only so close, and then the doors swing shut. It's a matter of trust, and you don't trust me."

She'd hurt him. She sat up beside him, drawing his discarded shirt up to her chin. "Calum, we've known each other just over a month—and you were gone for two weeks of it."

He stared at her over his shoulder. "And you wanted me when I got back. A woman doesn't give herself that way unless she cares, honey." Calum reached to take her hand and bring it to his lips. "I told you once that you'd see me coming the next time. Here."

"Calum . . ." She flushed, aware of how shy she was with him. Images of their loving danced in the firelight, along with images of his tenderness to her later. He'd just told her, in anger, that he loved her. . . .

He placed the wrapped package in her lap, watching her. "I wanted to give this to you last night. Open it."

Talia's hands shook as she unwrapped the package. Nestled in tissue was a beautiful Native American bag. Smooth, flat designs alternated with beads. Carefully folded beneath it was a beaded doeskin shift.

"The bag is decorated with porcupine quills and is called a parfleche bag. I want you to have it. It was Una's, a gift from her husband." Calum traced the beaded cerulean flowers. "This was Una's bridal dress. Sybil wore it, and I've asked for it until the next bride of the Tallchiefs accepts marriage."

"Oh, Calum, I couldn't possibly accept these. . . ." Talia dashed away the tears burning at her lids. "I've never cried so much since—"

Calum eased her into his lap and wrapped a blanket around her. She listened to the wind passing through the pines and to the beating of his heart. She felt so safe; she wouldn't have moved if she had the energy. "You are a persistent man,

Calum Tallchief. I sense that you operate by wearing people
down, or boxing them into situations. I do not like boxes,
though I am presently worn down. You have no idea what a
life with me could be like. You don't know what you're asking of me. I'm a contemporary woman, a free spirit. I could
never accept your basic warrior act and a structured life-
style."

"I'm asking you to trust me, honey."

She ran her finger down his bearded cheek. Calum kissed
her fingertip, his eyes dark and serious as they met hers. She
lifted her lips slightly to his and brushed a kiss across them.
"There are ways that I absolutely trust you."

She kissed the corner of his mouth, then the other. She eased
her fingers into the warm, sleek texture of his hair, tilted her
head slightly and fitted her mouth upon his. Calum tensed, but
held very still beneath her light kisses.

She allowed the blanket to fall aside and locked her arms
around his neck, pressing her body into his. She eased him
backward, aware suddenly of how easily a big man could be
moved when he wanted to be. Calum drew the sleeping bag up
to cover her back as she settled upon him. In his arms, she felt
warm and safe, and she knew that sleep had begun to enfold
her. "I'd like you to make love with me...." she heard herself whisper.

She heard his wistful groan before she drifted into sleep.

Talia awoke slowly, just as she was moving over Calum. His
hands were locked righteously on her waist. His lashes gleamed
in the firelight, shadowing his eyes. She touched his cheeks,
smoothed the dark beard and ran her fingertip across his
brows. His hair ran sleek and cool through her fingers as she
settled upon him, taking him within her slowly, as naturally as
she breathed his scent.

Calum held very still, his body taut, as his hands caressed
her hips, claiming them with splayed fingers. Then he moved
swiftly, easing her beneath him, filling her in one thrust. Talia
lifted her body to him, and then he was where she wanted
him—

His mouth took hers in the hungry way she wanted, and she
gave herself to the fire igniting between them.

She awoke the second time to find Calum fully dressed, braced against the saddle, his legs stretched out to the fire. Daylight had penetrated the top of the tepee, and the fire was dying between them. She met his dark gaze, felt the tug of desire, and something gentler, more frightening, stirred within her. A tiny spray of sparks shot between them, and she realized that tears were slowly falling from her cheeks. "What do you want from me, Calum?"

"Only what you want to give."

"The legend—the ring is meant for your true love, Calum. I can't wear it."

"Afraid? I didn't think you would be afraid of me, Petrovna. Or my love." His challenge curled, too softly, around her.

"You know very well that we are a bad mix. A combustible one."

"*Combustion.* That's a very apt word. So the way you see our relationship is that when you're ready to move on, that's it? You just take me when you want me? You set the terms?" He threw his coffee into the fire, creating a dying, hissing sound that matched the feeling in her heart.

Until she remembered that she had taken Calum too quickly, that his body had flowed deeply into hers, so perfectly that— Talia leaped to her feet, her head hit the tepee's canvas. She began hurriedly dressing, while Calum watched grimly. "Now what?"

"Oh, nothing," she returned airily, plopping down to lace up her boots. She glanced at him as he began to fold the bedding. She wanted to get away from him, to think; thinking near Calum seemed impossible, especially with the scents of their lovemaking enfolding her. His body smelled wonderful— Talia cleared her throat. "I think I'll just be going now. Thanks for everything."

His hand caught the back of her collar. "This is no have-me-and-leave-me hotel, honey. You are going back with me, Petrovna, sweetheart. The safe way."

"I sense that in some way I have upset your sensibilities, Mr. Tallchief."

"Always the last word, Petrovna?"

She opened her lips, but decided from the way Calum was looking down at her that perhaps, for this time alone, he could have the last word.

The next morning, Elspeth replaced the telephone in its cradle. Her classic black sweater displayed her willowy body, which flowed into a long wool skirt of the Tallchief plaid. "That was Sybil on the phone. She thinks that Calum was being high-handed in not letting us help take care of you last night. My brother probably hovered over your bed all night, just watching you breathe. To catch a cold with a Tallchief male around is no simple matter. Though I really wish you would have been here when Calum was so ill after the logrolling incident. Sybil is also very frustrated with Marcella Portway's missing royal Spanish gene. Marcella is determined that she has royal blood and a family castle somewhere in Spain. She doesn't want to believe that her ancestors were of the ordinary mix."

Talia pushed Marcella's desired genealogy away and cut to news of Calum. "Calum was ill?"

"He caught cold, and could have developed complications. When they're ill, all Tallchief males are horribly evil-tempered."

"I feel so guilty. He didn't tell me."

"He'll tell you what suits him."

Talia dealt with this news; she had caused Calum actual harm, and yet he had come after her, playing the Desert Hawk. Elspeth studied Talia beneath her lashes and traced the tiny rosebuds on her china cup. "So Calum took you to our parents' graves?" Elspeth asked quietly.

"Yes, this morning. It's so beautiful there in the meadow with the tall pines around, almost like a chapel. I felt as though Calum was sharing something precious with me. Oh, Elspeth, he was hurting so...all of you must have been devastated...Calum looked almost...like a little lost boy there in the snow by your parents' graves. I ached for him. All of you must have loved your parents deeply and still miss them." Calum's expression of deep grief had touched Talia, and she had moved close to him. His arm had come around her in a natural gesture, drawing her nearer.

The hours in Elspeth's home soothed Talia, who couldn't deal with Calum's cool, polite manners since he'd brought her back to his house. He'd gone off to chop firewood with his brothers. In his dark, ominous mood, she had no doubt that he was throwing tomahawks and running down game in his moccasins.

Talia inhaled the scent of herbal tea. "I'm very uncertain about this entire project. Calum is not an easy man to understand. For instance, how could he stop his entire career and decide to spend the winter at home?"

"Have you asked him?" Elspeth's black hair gleamed in the brilliant morning light. Her gray eyes were much softer than Calum's steel-shaded ones, yet Talia sensed that when Elspeth was tested, her Tallchief inheritance would hold like honed steel. Behind her stood Una's huge loom; on the floor sat a huge basket filled with yarns matching the Tallchief plaid. Lengths of dyed wool from the Tallchief Ranch's Scottish sheep hung from the wall in rich array.

The scent of herbs and baking bread blended with the harmony in Elspeth's quiet home. She had been studying Una's journals; they lay open on the table, along with Elspeth's notes.

Talia traced Una's script with her fingertip. She deeply loved the man who had captured her and whom she had tamed. "It is not easy to communicate with Calum. We've known each other only a short time."

"Una's legends were true enough with Duncan and Sybil. Once Sybil brought the Tallchief cradle to him, Megan's birth was certain. My stern, grim brother was destined for a household of women. He's their great big spoiled pet, and proud of them." Elspeth placed Talia's hands apart. She looped dark green yarn around them and began winding it into a ball as they talked.

"Which piece of Una's dowry have you claimed to return to the Tallchiefs?"

"A paisley shawl of fine merino wool, dark red, like coals lit by fiery tints of yellow and orange. Una describes its pattern and texture beautifully."

"And the legend?"

Elspeth flushed slightly and looked away. "There is something about the lady huntress taming a scarred warrior, and ice and fire. I haven't been able to read that part clearly yet, because of damage to the old pages. I'm not certain I want to. It definitely is more complex than the other legends. Una has blended it with a legend from our Sioux heritage."

She smiled quietly at Talia. "I've just started a new Tallchief pattern and need more yarn. Calum works regularly from his home. He helps regularly with the Tallchief Cattle Ranch and sheep shearing, and with wood gathering and with family events. For instance, before Megan was born, Calum cancelled everything and made her wear a beeper. Not only did Duncan carry one, but so did Calum and Birk. Poor Sybil was weighted down with every emergency contact device possible, including a flare signal. When she was allowed to drive by herself, my three brothers ran an ongoing spy mission, networking with the entire town and neighbors."

"I think you're being evasive about your legend and I think Calum can be very...centered."

"You mean when he wants something, he's very dedicated to obtaining it? Like a hunter." Elspeth avoided the return to her legend.

"Yes." Talia frowned at the rhythmic motion of Elspeth's hands. She fought the slow anger riding her; Calum would know about birth control, an important matter to be discussed by both participants. "He has old-fashioned ideas."

"My brothers are like that, especially when they care. They can be overpowering, just like our great-great-grandfather was with Una. They can be...devious."

"Devious. Like Calum's Desert Hawk. He still hasn't paid fully for that." Talia scowled at the journals.

"They are challenging." Elspeth finished the ball of yarn and studied Talia. "You realize that you're just exactly what Calum needed. He needed a good challenge, and the gossip in Amen Flats is that you are his fast game."

Elspeth smiled. "That was quite the sight—to see you riding on the back of Calum's horse, wrapped in a blanket against the cold and huddled to his back. The travois—the tent poles dragging behind the horse—carried the tepee and camping gear. The image dates back to Una and Tallchief's time, when he first captured her."

"Captured? You think Calum has captured a bride?"

"Umm . . . it was only an image, probably a false one." Elspeth's tone was noncommittal.

Talia remembered Calum's body lodged deeply within hers, the fire rising between them, the beating of their hearts— "You realize that he told me to stand and fight, don't you? What kind of a man would say that to a lady? To me, a Petrovna?"

With her hands free, she leaped to her feet and began to pace. Locked in her thoughts of Calum, Talia touched the huge old spinning wheel near a window cluttered with bundles of lavender and sage. "Now Calum has me sounding like Papa," she muttered.

Elspeth seemed lost in thought for a moment, then carefully placed the ball of yarn in the huge wooden bowl near the loom. "By the way, did you know that Calum is an expert climber? He was the only one qualified for the rescue operation."

"I wanted to think. He makes that difficult—" Talia rounded on Elspeth as the other woman elegantly poured tea. *"He climbs mountains? Rescue operation?"*

Elspeth's gray eyes met Talia's. "The climber who died had panicked. He was told to wait for Calum. He didn't. He fell to his death, right past Calum."

"You mean, he was fully qualified for rescue and he let me struggle up to grab his boot? He let me freeze on that sheer rock and didn't help?"

Elspeth's cool, amused look took in Talia's taut body, her flushed face and her furious expression. She stood up to take Talia's hands in her own. "Would you have wanted him to interfere? In some ways, you and he are alike . . . you like to do things your own way. Calum has traveled all over the world. He rescued Kadar's sister from an avalanche, and he's a

champion skier. He also reviews Broadway plays for critics
who can't. He's been searching for the best challenge yet. If
I'm not mistaken, he's found what he wants. What do you
think?"

"Calum reviews plays?" Talia ran through Calum's comments and weighed them. They were professional.

"Mmm ... He's led an interesting life." Elspeth smoothed
her sleek black chignon with an elegant hand. Then she smiled
warmly. "Interesting tidbits about my brother, eh?"

"I'd like to take his thick neck between my hands and—"
Talia stopped pacing back and forth in the serene kitchen. She
stared at Elspeth, who was standing hands on hips, legs spread.
Talia looked closely at Elspeth's grin. "You're enjoying this.
You're deliberately feeding me tidbits about Calum."

"Aye, captive bride of the Tallchief. That I am. I've had my
fill of Calum Tallchief, and it's time for another woman to
share that burden. He's told you he loves you, and you're on
the run. Get him to wear the Tallchief kilt. I'm counting on
your help, and don't listen to his moans about the cold wind
sweeping up his backside."

Elspeth smoothed her fingertip over the Tallchief plaid
neatly folded on her worktable. From beneath her glossy raven
lashes, she studied Talia's expression, and then Elspeth smiled
slightly. "The bridal tepee is a lovely Tallchief tradition, but I
really didn't know if Calum would—"

Talia rounded on her. *"Bridal tepee?"*

Ten

___

Freshly showered, Calum rinsed his old-fashioned straight razor in the bathroom sink. Electric razors served a purpose, but not for the heavy beard he had acquired in the past two days. Talia's climbing escapade, and the woodcutting and hauling, had prevented his usual ritual. He'd needed the physical exercise of chopping wood and hauling it to his home; he'd needed to think. In his home, Talia's jasmine scent prevented that. Now, with a better grip on his emotions, he'd planned a logical meeting of the minds with Talia, and, hopefully, a meeting of their bodies to confirm her agreement with him.

He met his reflection in the mirror and shook his head. A man couldn't haul his bridal tepee around forever, waiting for his chosen bride to decide to come to him. But that was exactly what he did, unfolding and establishing the whole process yet another time, deep in the woods of Tallchief Mountain. Life with Talia could exhaust a man in multiple ways. A woman of action needed adjustments in the courting game; for her, he was willing to skip certain pleasures, like conventional dating, for the present.

Calum ignored the small dollop of shaving cream that dropped onto his chest. A regular shaving time would be impossible with Talia nearby; he could cope with that easily, but not with the abrasions his beard left on her skin. He wiped the razor blade on the towel draped around his neck. He'd been a little evil-tempered with Talia. It wasn't every day that a meticulous man realized he was so stoned with love and passion that he'd forgotten to use protection. He'd fallen into Talia's tender hands like a ripe fruit, dismissing his plans to tell her about his feelings. The word *laid* taunted him.

He clung to the moment when she'd given herself to him, wrapped himself in that small security.

The squall of Talia's red sports car coming to a stop outside his home caused Calum to pause. Olaf, who had been curiously studying Calum's shaving techniques, bounded past him, followed by Ivana and Igor. Amid the hectic, happy barking of the puppy, who had begun imitating Olaf, the front door slammed. The sound of Talia's boots marched through the house. She paused in the kitchen. He frowned at his image in the mirror and began a slow, studious swipe up from his jaw, drawing away the white foam on his cheek. He smiled grimly, realizing how much he liked Talia hunting him, coming for him. This time he was ready.

Talia flung open the bathroom door, stepping into the room immediately. "Here you are! I read your comments, Mr. Professional Reviewer, Top Mountain Climber, Champion Skier, and I—"

She blinked; her gaze jerked down his body. "Calum. You are shaving in the nude."

"True," he returned pleasantly, and continued shaving.

Determined to shoot at him whatever was nettling her, Talia continued, "I've just come from Elspeth, and—"

"And?" Calum patted away the remaining foam and turned to her. After a lifetime of Elspeth's delicate manipulation, Calum had known she would intervene in his romance of Talia. He'd known it from Elspeth's first approving "Aye!" He braced himself....

Her eyes skipped down to his arousal and widened. "Uh . . . I'll talk with you later."

Calum threw the towel around his neck to the floor in one swift, impatient movement. "I've got plans for later. You're on my schedule *now*, dear heart."

"You brought a bridal tepee up to the mountain. Everyone saw us come down." She backed up as he advanced a step. "What plans?"

Calum took another step. "It's called tradition, sweetheart. Much to my amazement, I've found that I'm a traditional man where you're concerned. You're the only woman who has mattered to me enough to admit that I am not a contemporary man. I had planned a romantic evening the night before, which frightened you. It seemed a shame to waste a pot of good clam chowder, so I decided you might want something hot at the end of your, what?—caper?—in freezing weather?"

"You did all that work for clam chowder?" She backed up against the wall. "Just what are your plans for later?"

Calum leaned down to place his cheek along hers. His body hummed with the need to hold her, yet he feared frightening her. He was afraid enough for both of them. He nuzzled, then gently bit her ear. "Romancing my bride in my own time. Without her skipping from A to Z and seducing me before I'm ready. You move too fast, Petrovna. I fell into your hands like a ripe fruit up on the mountain. Do you know how I feel about that? I'll tell you."

Talia trembled. She shook her head. "I'm not really a very good housekeeper, you know. I just stayed to irritate you, and— Oh, by the way, I found the envelope of your suggestions on the kitchen table. Thank you for the wonderful helpful hints on *Nachos and Nanette*. . . ."

Her breath caught as the tip of his tongue toyed with her ear. "Petrovna, shut up. I had major plans for the use of the bridal tepee, which you squashed. You frightened me badly by climbing up that cliff. Then you had me. I was shocked and not in a pleasant mood when I realized you'd struck again. Counted coup and had me, laid me out and took me, before I could explain exactly how I feel. A bridal tepee is not the place

for anger, which you had aroused in me. That is why I didn't
pursue my plans for the tepee further. Take a note, Petrovna.
Not only did I forget protection—something I've never done
before—there's tradition. Courtship. Rules and terms. A
woman like you could emasculate an unsuspecting man.''

"Not you," she breathed unevenly after a quick glance
downward. Calum allowed his masculinity to lurch heavily
against her stomach, which she sucked in instantly. "You're
tender and considerate and... You forgot protection? I mean,
a methodical man like you—that discovery alone must have
been shattering. An untied end, so to speak. Do you love me?"
she asked hurriedly.

"Enough to try again, which any man with good sense
wouldn't do. Let me phrase this very carefully, Petrovna. You
could be carrying my baby. How do you feel about that?"

When her shock turned to surprised wonder, he pounced.
"You're a quick mover. It would be just like you to take what
I've given no other woman and create a child before our relationship is thoroughly resolved. I can deal with that compli-
cation. In fact, I welcome the possibility. If you do."

He proceeded quickly, before his dreams could consume
him. Before he could pick her up, close to his heart, and race
up the stairs with her. "You move fast, and I'm trying to catch
you on the run. I want you to know that the lack of preven-
tion *wasn't* on purpose. That I am not trying an old trick that
my great-great-grandfather probably used to keep Una."

Her hand went up to his cheek. Her eyes were gentle upon
him. "Why, Calum. You've shocked yourself. You're in a stew
as to how to handle me and the situation."

"I have a backup plan, Petrovna. Logic always prevails. I
want you to know that from now on, I will always be very
careful with you in every way."

Talia eased slightly away from him and out into the hallway. "Calum, you could, ah...catch cold. Exactly what are
your plans for tonight?"

"I would like, with your cooperation, to begin the basis of
a long-term relationship. I want to romance my bride and tell
her what is in my heart. Like the first step in negotiating a
lasting proposition." He let her feed on that as she took on

step backward and hit the stairway. "Keep in mind, Petrovna, that you are a fast-moving woman. I am just doing my best to cope."

She took a step up, her eyes on a level with his. "I sense that you are very fragile right now."

He snorted in disbelief, and she took another step. His eyes jerked to her breasts, rising and falling within the tight black sweater. He could almost taste the delicate nubs, the softness cupped by his hand. "I feel as hard as iron," he stated with confidence. He asked again the question she had not answered. "How would you feel if you found you were carrying my child?"

"Tallchief, I took you because I wanted you. Is this an even-Steven sort of gig? Where, ah . . . you would like to repay certain, ah . . . scores?"

"I am not going to throw my love at you like an old shoe, if that's what you mean." A trickle of anger ran through Calum as he recalled what she had said. "You were right. I should have picked a better way of telling you. It's not a phrase I've used often."

She continued to back up the stairs as Calum advanced upward. "Okay—here's how I felt. I felt you . . . pulsing in me, so deep that I didn't know where I stopped and you began. You completed me and I completed you. We were one. I thought then, 'How marvelous . . . how wonderful . . . You are mine, Calum Tallchief. This is beautiful.' And then I realized I was crying with the beauty of it, a timeless essence of how life goes on . . . of what you gave to me, and how I wanted to protect and nourish your gift."

Her softly spoken words stunned him in midstep, wrapped around his heart and hugged him. He forced away his light-headed joy and proceeded. "Will you be my bride tonight? Will you let me tell you the things that are in my heart?"

In the shadows, she met his eyes. "I am so afraid, Calum. I thought I could handle my emotions. Where you're concerned, I can't."

"Share them with me." Upstairs now, Calum cradled her cheeks in his hands. "Make me a part of you tonight, Talia."

She closed her eyes, tears spiking her lashes. "It is important to you that . . . we use the tepee?"

He would not lie to her, as badly as he wanted the night to tell her of his heart. "It is important. But we can stay here. Or I will leave you alone. You decide."

Her lips trembled, and still she did not meet his eyes. "You are so . . . traditional."

"It is my wedding night. One like I haven't had before. Nor will I again. Come with me."

"Yes," she whispered unevenly, so quietly he had to lean close to hear. "Yes, I'll come with you."

"Love is a circle," Calum whispered unevenly when she stood in the tepee's firelight, clad in the doeskin shift.

He tossed away the warm sweat suit and maxicoat that she had worn riding on the horse behind him. Calum quickly stripped away his own clothing; the stone lay warm upon his chest. He stood very straight, letting her see his obvious need of her. The ceremony was age-old, that of a man and woman coming together, knowing that their lives would forever be intertwined, as their bodies soon would be.

With her hair undone and loose around the shift, Talia allowed Calum to replace the garnet ring to her finger. The tent billowed with the night wind that sighed in the pine boughs overhead. "Why do you want me?" she asked quietly, as Calum brought their joined hands to his lips.

"You make my heart glad. You fill me with wonder and joy."

"You haven't asked me to say I love you."

"That has to come from your heart. What you give me now is enough."

The doeskin fringes fell away from her arms as Calum lifted one; he brushed a kiss on the inside of her elbow. In this moment, Talia's eyes softened upon him, stroking his face with a tenderness he hoped to nurture. "Come to me," he whispered as her trembling fingertips brushed his lips.

He lightly kissed her forehead, her eyebrows, her lashes, and straightened, easing away from her. Talia's eyes shimmered in the firelight. "You make me feel like I'm shining, Calum."

He feared she would change her mind, but then she lifted the shift slowly and discarded it. Talia's long, pale limbs gleamed in the firelight as she slowly lowered herself onto the bed he had prepared of soft old quilts, sewn by his mother and grandmothers. Talia's movements stirred the scents of sweet grass he had placed beneath the pallet; he caught her jasmine fragrance and her exotic, intimate womanly scent.

Calum stood still, absorbing the picture of her hair, flowing over the pillows and the warm soft quilts, over her shoulders. He prayed there would be other times, but this one would be locked in his heart with their first loving.

"Come to me, Calum," she whispered above the sound of the fire and the drumming of his heart.

He came with purpose and touched her reverently, lightly. First her face, brushing her lips with kisses, then her throat. She trembled as he touched her breasts, his rugged face warm and strong against her throat, his kisses heating her skin. She waited, breathing unevenly, washed by emotions of joy and of fear. She curbed her need to take him quickly as Calum eased her fully into his arms, a gentle abrasion of rough skin against her own. Of his heat and his length stroking her thigh.

Beneath her palms, Calum's back rippled as he moved over her very carefully, fitting his length to her.

She respected his need for tradition, for this moment, letting him lead her.

Calum rested above her, his eyes light within his tanned, rugged face and the scented shadows. Braced on his forearms, he smoothed a strand of hair from her cheek. His expression was tender, yet fiercely proud, his fingers trembling as they stroked her cheek.

Talia dived into the sensations he arose within her, the tenderness she felt for him now. The joy for what would come. She eased her thighs apart, admitting him to the cradle of her body. He waited, his heart pounding against hers, his body taut. Their eyes locked as she moved her hips, lifted to receive him, and he slid home, deep within her.

For long heartbeats, he lay very still, stretching her to the limits, easing deeper. He filled her with himself and with the wonder of the marriage ritual.

The elemental ceremony caused her to cry out, a tear sliding from her cheek. He kissed away the dampness and laid his head down beside hers. "Listen to our hearts," he whispered against her hot skin. "We are one."

He moved slowly, thoroughly, within her, and the storm crashed within them, flinging them into the heat and the thunder. When she burst, she held to Calum, gradually floating back to the safety of the soft old quilts scented of sweet grass. She dozed and awoke to his cleansing, his tenderness.

His radiant grin took her heart and stunned her for a heartbeat. She grinned back. "Taking a captive groom isn't that hard."

"Isn't it? Now that sounds like a challenge, honey." Then he bent to kiss her in a shocking place. While she dealt with that tender assault, he licked her navel, then found her breasts. Calum took one into his mouth, suckling deeply, alternating with gentle bites.

While the first joining had been dreamlike and beautiful, Talia sensed that he no longer needed to observe tradition. She held his head to her, heard his hungry sounds of pleasure. The delicate pressure caught fire, cords heating throughout her body, lodging deep within a place Calum had just filled. Her body tightened desperately, and she knew that this was the mating of bodies, as well as hearts and souls.

Calum trimmed the shocking, primitive needs enticing her body. He kissed her hungrily, his tongue finding hers, drawing it into his lips to suckle. She tasted him, locked her hands to his strong shoulders and allowed herself to fly. His body flowed against hers, tormenting, heating, retreating.

She pushed against him, locked her arms around his neck and bit him. "You're not going anywhere, Calum Tallchief. Not now."

He laughed aloud, startling her. The deep rumbling sound vibrated against her breasts, sensitized by his tender treatment. Talia bent to find his nipples, suckling the flat, hard nubs. She grinned against his chest as Calum groaned hungrily, his tall, strong body hers to tempt and to heat. She licked his navel and Calum's big hands locked to her head, drawing her upward for his openmouthed kiss. "Take it easy, Petrovna."

Raw emotion coursed through his deep, uneven tone. She had him now; he was her game, her captive. She moved her leg over him experimentally, allowing her heat to warm his hard thigh. Calum's hand found her then, his palm caressing her in gentle circles. She flowed against him and nipped his nipple again. His ragged groan was a sharp protest, his body taut against hers.

Calum's fingers slid to caress her. He touched her and she bloomed, heated and moist, at his stroke. He nourished a tender bit within her, slowly, delicately, and Talia began to vibrate, her blood pounding. "Calum?"

"You are so hot, vibrating with heat—" When she would have taken him, Calum resisted, smoothing her body with big, strong hands. He took her hips within his hands, cradled her against him and rocked gently, undulating against her.

The tiny contractions caught Talia unaware, lifting her higher, and she gripped his shoulders tightly as her body was riveted on a peak she didn't understand. When she could breathe again, she met Calum's teasing kisses and opened her eyes to see his tender smile. "You think this is funny, Tallchief?"

"Beautiful. I think you are beautiful." His fingers stroked her again, and a tiny convulsion of pleasure raced through her, causing her to gasp.

Calum raised her fingers to suckle them, his gaze locked with hers. Talia reached lower to touch him, and Calum held very still as she fitted her hand around him. "Don't," he ordered rawly as she began to experiment. "Just don't."

He fused his mouth to hers, and she took. She lost a sense of tomorrow or yesterday and found only pleasure in looking at him. "Tell me what you like."

"I love you, Petrovna. All of you. You fascinate me. Each moment with you is exciting. But if you mean in relation to this—" His hands swept meaningfully over her body, drawing her close to him. "Your breasts. They fascinate me."

He turned her over to study them. Then bent to kiss the tip of each one. "They're pink and soft and tasty."

Riveted by his expression, Talia forgot her shyness. He caressed her aching breasts equally and placed his splayed fingers over her soft stomach. "I like this. It's gurgly and warm and—"

His hand slid lower, curving over her. His expression was changing intensely. "You're fragrant here, honey. Like a flower."

"That's how I feel when you touch me...like a flower opening, becoming beautiful," she admitted shyly.

"Petal by petal..." Calum stroked her lightly, and she bloomed beneath his touch.

He trembled, desire sharpening his features, his hair disheveled by her fingers. He eased over her, drawing her knees high to kiss the tender insides.

He slid to fill her, and she cried out, locking him to her. He pushed deeper, his breath warm against her cheek, her throat. She turned to meet his hungry kiss, and the words flowed from her lips to his. "Calum. Calum. Calum. I love you."

The fierce pounding of their hearts rose and heated and thundered through their pleasure. Calum bound her to him with strong arms, and she captured him with her limbs and her mouth fused to his. They moved higher in the incredible pleasure, found each other and cried out. Her shattering was followed by his, and she heard his muffled shout. Talia smiled against Calum's shoulder as his body pulsed deeply within her. She'd taken him, and with an age-old wisdom, Talia realized that they had bonded, mated, in a way she would never forget.

"Stop smirking, honey," Calum muttered drowsily against her throat.

She stroked his tall body, relaxed now upon her. He was vulnerable now, hers to protect. "Shh... Go to sleep."

Calum eased slightly aside, but stayed locked within her.

During the night, he stirred, filling her once more, and Talia rose to meet him. "I love you," she cried out, taking him fiercely.

* * *

Calum listened to the silence of his house. They had returned home midmorning on the second day. After their hurried shower—Calum really enjoyed that shower, with the water
sluicing between them as they made love—Talia had kissed
him, dressed and soared out of the driveway in her red car.
She'd been humming, ready to capture the world and to redo
her play. Calum had unpacked, started lunch and laundry,
then settled down to catch up on his messages and accounts.

Olson's redemption was progressing according to plan. His
wife had tied him to the rack, and he was definitely paying.
Calum smiled at Olson's dropping bank account balance.
Calum had gotten the bank's permission to "audit anytime"
when he worked for them. He tapped out a computer note to
Olson's private machine—"I'm watching."

He found another message waiting for Olson and scanned
it. "You jerk. Keep your hands in your own pockets, lover boy.
Big Sister is watching." Calum grimly erased Talia's message;
Olson just might match his ex-secretary to Calum's new bride.
The tenderness in their bridal tent, and Talia's crying out her
love for him, were not going to be disturbed. Calum wanted
everything running smoothly.

As smoothly as possible, with a volatile, unpredictable
woman like Talia.

Calum checked on Sybil's progress in locating another
Tallchief cradle; the Sioux warrior had built and sold others to
support his growing family. She muttered about Marcella
Portway's missing Spanish royal gene and said she'd locate a
cradle soon, running through old auction summaries and antique stores' inventories.

Freed from Ivana and Igor, who were curled together,
sleeping, Olaf placed his head on Calum's knee. He whined
softly and Calum rubbed his ears. "I miss her, too. It's a one-
step-at-a-time proposition with Petrovna, soon to be Tallchief. I intend to romance her out of those Hessian boots and
add a wedding ring to Una's Celtic band. We've got all winter."

"I love you. . . ." Talia had cried out, her body throbbing
against his.

Calum inhaled, realizing that his loins were indeed old-fashioned and lust-prone when he thought of Talia—the woman he considered his wife. There was more, of course, an emotion that ran on a level that bonded heart and soul when the heat had passed.

Calum realized that he was slightly and old-fashionedly shocked by Talia's volcanic response to him. He hadn't known how much had been missing from his marriage. The completion was there, the feeling that the circle was completed when he lay in her arms. When they talked softly, or played.

He realized he was grinning like a boy. Talia caused him to feel that way—light, young, carefree. He'd told her about the Tallchiefs' struggle to keep together as orphans. She'd understood and told him about her "long white dress phobia."

They were communicating, and everything was proceeding along nicely.

Talia stepped into his office and found him sitting at his computer. Their eyes locked; she walked toward him in the long-legged, hip-swaying slow walk that dried his throat. Her short skirt flared as she eased her leg over to straddle him in the chair. "Hello, darlin'. Doing your methodical investment thing?"

"I checked on your freewheeling investments. You're an intuitive player, and a good one." Calum found her moist and hot to his touch. "You do everything well."

"Why, thank you, darlin'. It's nice to know I'm appreciated." Her tights tore in his hand as Talia ran her hands over his cheeks. "I miss the beard," she whispered huskily. Then she bent to nibble on his jaw, his throat, and took away his breath when she suckled him.

With a new confidence, she found his confined desire, stroked him lightly and tugged open his zipper.

When Calum could speak again, his heart pounding like a running stag, and Talia had wilted warmly upon him, he muttered.

She forced her head up to kiss his jaw. "Mmm?"

"Ambushed again." He lowered her to the floor and began slowly unbuttoning her sweater. "Let's take it slower this time."

"You'll have to keep up. I am a woman of action—" She inhaled as he began to kiss her throat and breasts. Her fingertips dug into his shoulders and she bit his neck gently as he proceeded to pleasure her. "Oh, my...Calum, you are a thorough man."

"Mmm...I manage to get there, honey."

She fluttered her lashes against his throat. "I've got news for you, darlin'. Calum the cool has got to go. The name no longer applies."

Eleven

————

The first week of December, the curtain came down on the last act of *Nachos and Nanette*'s first night. Talia held her breath; the audience rose to its feet, clapping and whistling. She beamed, elated—her first play was a success, thanks to Calum's well-placed criticism. She'd touched the hearts of cowboys and ranchers and farm wives and merchants. The local undertaker wore a grin. A section of stern-faced Native Americans had nodded their approval.

Life in a small town wasn't that bad.

Waking up in Calum's arms was fantastic.

Lounging in his shirt and socks and arguing over who read the comics first was quite pleasant.

She hadn't thought that a traditional man would play house-husband while she worked to perfect the play. Calum practically dressed her in the morning and tucked her into bed at night. He listened and encouraged and saw that she ate regular meals; he'd handled her business investments that needed immediate attention. He'd pacified her family, promising to bring her home soon. His foot massages were wonderful. Tonight he understood her fear of failure, her need to wear her battle gear, the black sweater and tight pants and Hessian boots. He'd even polished them for her, along with his Western boots; Megan had helped by drooling upon the leather.

When Talia was discouraged about the play, he'd known just how to challenge her. When the applause began, he had vanished from his seat. Everything was perfect—she wanted to share her victory with Calum Tallchief.

She'd find him, drag him into a locked closet and toss up his kilt. Talia hurried down the hallway to the reception room and flung open the door.

The Tallchief clan stood together, dressed in white ruffled shirts, kilts and the Fearghus-Tallchief plaid draped from shoulder to hip. Elspeth, looking very feminine, stood in front of her tall, grim brothers. Sybil held Duncan's hand, a smile touching her lips, her eyes warm upon him. In Birk's arms, Megan was a miniature replica of the Tallchiefs, with her gray eyes and glossy black hair. Birk didn't mind the wet spot on his shoulder from Megan's nibbles, a child teething on loved ones. Lacey, looking like a Scots elf amid the towering Tallchiefs, grinned up at the males' glowering expressions.

Calum walked slowly toward Talia, a tall, dark man with fierce, stormy gray eyes.

The pure white of his shirt contrasted with his dark skin, the ruffles a contrast against his rugged face, the dragon green and Tallchief vermilion catching the overhead light. His jet-black hair gleamed; her fingers recognized the crisp texture, the way it curved on his nape. His shoulders, broad beneath the layers of shirt and plaid, blocked out the soft, knowing smiles of the other Tallchiefs. The kilt moved around his long legs, sheathed in plaid stockings.

"Aye!" the Tallchiefs shouted cheerily behind him. "Aye!"

His hand stretched out to her, large and callused. Strong enough to keep her. Gentle enough to exquisitely pleasure her.

His steady smoke-gray eyes held hers. He came to claim her as his bride, with a binding legality this time. To change the present, to take her to the future. To place a gold band beside the garnets she wore, to make her his... To make her a part of

him and the Tallchiefs. To transport her into age-old
traditions, into a love that frightened her to her very core.

Battered by her old fears, her uncertainties and her new love,
Talia reacted instinctively to protect herself. She fled down the
hallway and hurled herself up the stairs to the rooftop.

The cold December wind hit her, taking away her breath.
She leaped to another building, keeping to the shadows of a
chimney. Then she hurried across the night shadows to a flat
building, dropped to the fire escape and ran down it. Ten feet
from the street, she held the bars and dropped gracefully to the
ground.

A horse moved from the night shadows into the light of a
street lamp. Calum sat in the saddle, still dressed in his ruffled shirt, plaid and kilt. "Having a nice time?" he asked in
too soft a voice.

"Oh, hello, Calum." She began walking hurriedly on the
sidewalk, the hoofbeats sounding behind her.

"Talia." Her name echoed like a shot in a showdown.

She pivoted on him, tears streaming down her face, emotions ripping through her. Against the night sky, he looked as
huge as some dark knight coming to claim her. Talia dashed
away her tears and backed away from his approaching horse.
"I'm scared," she admitted, shaking violently.

"No one said this would be easy."

She tried to find comfort in his tone, and couldn't; it lay
hard as steel between them. She could accept him, love him,
trust him...or she could walk away. Calum Tallchief tossed
the challenge at her without giving an inch. He sat in the saddle, the winter wind rippling his shirt and plaid and kilt.

She wore his family ring; it gleamed in the night as she held
up her hand protectively. Calum wanted to place another band
on her finger; he wanted more....

"I love you, Calum Tallchief." She dashed away the tears
freezing to her cheeks. She wanted him to scoop her up, warm
her and tell her that he loved her in that sweet, dark, hungry
way of his.

"Oh, Calum. I do love you," she whispered to the freezing
night wind, and realized that she was crying, her fist pressed
to her lips, her body trembling.

He'd left the choice to her....

* * *

The second week of December, Calum walked through Denver's elegant downtown section. Past the buildings and the streetlights overhead, the stars twinkled on the velvet night. A week without Talia grated on his sleepless nights.

He'd placed his love at her feet. He'd taken a chance that she loved him enough to step over the bridges that separated them; he'd meet her more than halfway.

Calum tugged up his black leather jacket collar against the biting wind. He dreaded Christmas more than ever, an outcast from the dreams he savored of Talia snug in his arms, laughing up at him, the future spreading before them.

"Aye!" The Tallchief cry echoed in the deserted streets, the cheery Christmas decorations mocking him from shop windows. He'd wanted to woo her in his arms, to gently ease her into the idea that he wanted the years with her.

Calum glared at the elves in a window, working to wrap presents for under the Christmas tree. In his heart, he was a married man, yet she'd nicked his pride. Her dismissal of commitment, of designing a future together, had wounded him.

"Aye!" His family had flopped out his intentions too quickly and frightened Talia. He'd read the fear widening her eyes, causing her face to pale.

His heart had shattered, tumbling down his damned kilt to his feet, when he saw Talia run from him. He'd give her only so much time, and then—

Calum noted a shadow sliding alongside his, a slender, agile shadow, and his hopes leaped by twenty stories.

He strolled into a darkened alley, and the shadow followed. A hard object pushed against his back. "Put your hands against that wall and spread 'em."

Calum obeyed, his palms flat on the building's bricks, and waited as the scent of jasmine curled around him. A soft hand brushed the nape of his neck; bangle bracelets chimed by his ear. "Don't get any ideas about turning around. Hold still while I frisk you."

"I might not have what you want." Calum tensed as two hands cupped his buttocks and squeezed gently.

"Oh, you do. An ample amount." A slender, pale hand slid to his chest, three garnets set in a Celtic design gleaming in the dim light. They disappeared beneath his sweater and grasped the polished stone around his throat. When her fingers released the stone, they slid in a caress across his chest and slowly down to his stomach.

Calum's heart kicked into double time when Talia's softness gently nudged his back and slid upward until her lips bit his ear. "Hold very still. Don't get any ideas that you can get away from me now."

He braced himself against a trail of kisses down his throat, and the feminine hands splayed possessively over his flat stomach. They slid lower, circled his waist and slid up inside his jacket to caress his taut back. She eased against his body, and nudged him with her hips. "Don't you dare move, Calum Tallchief. I've got you now. You are mine, darlin'."

She hugged him fiercely, and when Calum started to move, she tucked a small box into the front of his belt. He slowly took his shaking hands from the brick wall and opened the velvet box. A man's broad wedding band gleamed on the red cloth. "I love you, Calum Tallchief. You're just old-fashioned enough to consider this a dowry. Petrovna's Law. Equal terms. Are you going to stand and fight, or—"

Calum pivoted, clasped her in his arms and lifted her until her toes dangled inches above the street. Talia hurled her arms around his neck, her legs around his hips, and kissed him breathless. She leaned back momentarily to remove his steamed glasses and tuck them in his pocket.

"I've been taking lambada lessons," Calum said between hungry, teasing kisses. He'd noted Talia practicing as she cooked. The notion of dancing the sexy Latin-American steps with her pleased him, as she did. He gently squeezed her soft hips in his palms. She was wearing her black outfit, her Hessian boots locked firmly around his hips. That was good. When this lady came calling in Hessian boots, she meant business.

"I know. I've been tracking you. You need lots of practice. You need a dance partner who will keep you on your toes and not mind your nasty temper. One who will stand and fight you when you get overbearing and too traditional.''

"Mmm... Private lessons?"

"Very private. Tell me why you want me?'' Talia's husky question revealed her vulnerability to the commitment she had made to him tonight.

He kissed the sensitive corners of her mouth. "Because of your passion. Because of how you make me feel. Because of how my heart lifts just looking at you, you irritating little witch. You make me happy.''

For a moment, she just stared at him. "It's a circle, isn't it, Calum. You complete me, love.'' Talia ran her fingertips across his lips, her eyes glowing up at him. "It all happened so fast... I should have trusted you.... I realized later how much I hurt you when I ran—''

"Shh... You're here now. I love you, Talia.'' He kissed the tip of her nose, the damp spikes of her lashes.

Talia cradled his face in her hands, her thumbs brushing his lips. She looked at him with soft, glowing love. "You're my great adventure, my exciting challenge for the rest of our lives. You're my nerd, my Desert Hawk, my cowboy, my warrior, my friend...and, best of all, my love. Will you wear my ring? Will you marry me, Calum Tallchief?''

He fused his mouth to hers and held her close to his racing heart. "Figure it out.''

Breathless and soft against him, Talia smoothed his cheek. "There you go...challenging me. Take me somewhere where I can help you make up your mind. I want the whole works, the bridal gown and the hungry groom. I want my bridal tent after a wedding in which Petrovna and Tallchief men will probably shock the guests. I want to see my mother's face when she cries, and I want to cry at our children's weddings. I want to see my father slightly tipsy and boasting what a fine catch his little girl brought home. Alek and Anton will be grim at first, and no doubt run you through some ceremonial male gauntlet—''

Talia lifted her face to Calum's lips. He kissed away her tears, her friend, her lover. She kissed his lashes and found

them damp, this gentle, emotional, traditional man whom she
loved. "Tell me the legend again...."

Calum held her closer, this woman he loved and who loved
him in return. Against her lips, he whispered tenderly, "When
a man of Fearghus blood places the ring upon the right woman's finger, he'll capture his true love forever."

"It's true. Forever, my love." Their eyes met and promised.

The bloodred stones on the golden ring gleamed on Talia's
finger as she stroked Calum's tanned cheek. "So, my loving,
traditional husband-to-be, what do you know about seeds?"

He blinked, refocused and shook his head. "Seeds?"

Elspeth ran her fingertip across a pine bough laden with
snow. She gathered the Tallchief plaid shawl around her
against the winter night. Tallchief Mountain loomed above the
moon-trail on the lake. Circles were age-old, binding the past
and the future. Calum's circle was complete; his heart had
claimed another who loved him just as much. Elspeth inhaled
the scent of smoke and pine; the wind fluttered the tendrils
around her face, they clung to her skin. Duncan and Calum
had found their heart mates, their souls wedded for eternity.
Calum had another Tallchief cradle hidden away for the time
when it was needed. He would cry unashamedly then, a warrior humbled by his blood's continuing, by the woman who
loved him and who gave his child life.

From the mist upon the cattails and reeds swirled a warmer
wind; it circled Elspeth, toyed with the glossy black ends of her
twin braids and caressed her cheek. She nuzzled the Tallchief
plaid, her lips curving. Another love would be coming soon.
Which Tallchief would it seek?

"Aye," she whispered softly to the shadows. "Aye."

* * * * *

**In February, Silhouette Books is proud
to present the sweeping, sensual new novel
by bestselling author**

CAIT LONDON

about her unforgettable family—*The Tallchiefs.*

**TALLCHIEF
FOR KEEPS**

Everyone in Amen Flats, Wyoming, was talking about
Elspeth Tallchief. How she wasn't a thirty-three-year-old
virgin, after all. How she'd been keeping herself warm at
night all these years with a couple of secrets. And now one
of those secrets had walked right into town, sending
everyone into a frenzy. But Elspeth knew he'd come for
the *other* secret....

"Cait London is an irresistible storyteller..."
—*Romantic Times*

Don't miss TALLCHIEF FOR KEEPS by Cait London, available
at your favorite retail outlet in February from

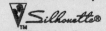

Look us up on-line at: http://www.romance.net

CLST

MILLION DOLLAR SWEEPSTAKES
AND EXTRA BONUS PRIZE DRAWING

No purchase necessary. To enter the sweepstakes, follow the directions published and complete and mail your Official Entry Form. If your Official Entry Form is missing, or you wish to obtain an additional one (limit: one Official Entry Form per request, one request per outer mailing envelope) send a separate, stamped, self-addressed #10 envelope (4 1/8" x 9 1/2") via first class mail to: Million Dollar Sweepstakes and Extra Bonus Prize Drawing Entry Form, P.O. Box 1867, Buffalo, NY 14269-1867. Request must be received no later than January 15, 1998. For eligibility into the sweepstakes, entries must be received no later than March 31, 1998. No liability is assumed for printing errors, lost, late, non-delivered or misdirected entries. Odds of winning are determined by the number of eligible entries distributed and received.

Sweepstakes open to residents of the U.S. (except Puerto Rico), Canada and Europe who are 18 years of age or older. All applicable laws and regulations apply. Sweepstakes offer void wherever prohibited by law. Values of all prizes are in U.S. currency. This sweepstakes is presented by Torstar Corp., its subsidiaries and affiliates, in conjunction with book, merchandise and/or product offerings. For a copy of the Official Rules governing this sweepstakes, send a self-addressed, stamped envelope (WA residents need not affix return postage) to: MILLION DOLLAR SWEEPSTAKES AND EXTRA BONUS PRIZE DRAWING Rules, P.O. Box 4470, Blair, NE 68009-4470, USA.

SWP-ME96

A Funny Thing Happened on the Way to the Baby Shower…

When four college friends reunite to celebrate the arrival of one bouncing baby, they find four would-be grooms on the way!

Don't miss a single, sexy tale in

RAYE MORGAN'S

Only in

BABY DREAMS
in May '96 (SD #997)

A GIFT FOR BABY
in July '96 (SD #1010)

BABIES BY THE BUSLOAD
in September '96 (SD #1022)

And look for

INSTANT DAD, WILL TRAIN
in November '96

Only from

RMBS

As seen on TV!
Free Gift Offer

With a Free Gift proof-of-purchase from any Silhouette® book, you can receive a beautiful cubic zirconia pendant.

This gorgeous marquise-shaped stone is a genuine cubic zirconia——accented by an 18" gold tone necklace.

(Approximate retail value $19.95)

Send for yours today...
compliments of ▼ *Silhouette*®
™

To receive your free gift, a cubic zirconia pendant, send us one original proof-of-purchase, photocopies not accepted, from the back of any Silhouette Romance™, Silhouette Desire®, Silhouette Special Edition®, Silhouette Intimate Moments® or Silhouette Yours Truly™ title available in August, September or October at your favorite retail outlet, together with the Free Gift Certificate, plus a check or money order for $1.65 U.S./$2.15 CAN. (do not send cash) to cover postage and handling, payable to Silhouette Free Gift Offer. We will send you the specified gift. Allow 6 to 8 weeks for delivery. Offer good until October 31, 1996 or while quantities last. Offer valid in the U.S. and Canada only.

Free Gift Certificate

Name: _____

Address: _____

City: _____ State/Province: _____ Zip/Postal Code: _____

Mail this certificate, one proof-of-purchase and a check or money order for postage and handling to: SILHOUETTE FREE GIFT OFFER 1996. In the U.S.: 3010 Walden Avenue, P.O. Box 9077, Buffalo NY 14269-9077. In Canada: P.O. Box 613, Fort Erie, Ontario L2Z 5X3.

FREE GIFT OFFER   084-KMD

ONE PROOF-OF-PURCHASE

To collect your fabulous FREE GIFT, a cubic zirconia pendant, you must include this original proof-of-purchase for each gift with the properly completed Free Gift Certificate.

084-KMD

The Calhoun Saga continues...

in November
New York Times bestselling author

NORA ROBERTS

takes us back to the Towers and introduces us to
the newest addition to the Calhoun household,
sister-in-law Megan O'Riley in

MEGAN'S MATE
(Intimate Moments #745)

And in December
look in retail stores for the special collectors'
trade-size edition of

THE
Calhoun
Women

containing all four fabulous Calhoun series books:
COURTING CATHERINE,
A MAN FOR AMANDA, FOR THE LOVE OF LILAH
and *SUZANNA'S SURRENDER.*
Available wherever books are sold.

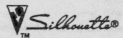

Look us up on-line at: http://www.romance.net

CALHOUN

You're About to Become a

Privileged
Woman

Reap the rewards of fabulous free gifts and benefits with proofs-of-purchase from Silhouette and Harlequin books

Pages & Privileges™

It's our way of thanking you for buying our books at your favorite retail stores.

PROOF OF PURCHASE
SD-PP172
Offer expires October 31, 1996

**Harlequin and Silhouette—
the most privileged readers in the world!**

For more information about Harlequin and Silhouette's PAGES & PRIVILEGES program call the Pages & Privileges Benefits Desk: 1-503-794-2499

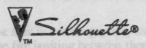

SD-PP172